HIRED HANDS

Edited by Winston Gieseke

HIRED HANDS

Gay Erotic Stories

BRUNO GMÜNDER

1st edition
© 2014 Bruno Gmünder Group GmbH
Kleiststraße 23-26, D-10787 Berlin
info@brunogmuender.com

Cover design: Dolph Caesar
Cover photo: © 2014 George Duroy, USA
belamionline.com (Model: Jim Kerouac)
Printed in Germany

ISBN 978-3-86787-787-9

More about our books and authors:
www.brunogmuender.com

CONTENTS

INTRODUCTION:
A HARD DAY'S WORK

You're alone. You're horny. And he's right there … the hunky handyman, the gorgeous gardener, the sexy stud washing the windows … You hadn't known he was so hot when you hired him, but now you can't take your eyes off him.

And then you notice he's looking back. Smiles are exchanged, and you shoot him a look that says it's OK to break from his duties. There's a more important service you need him to perform. On you. He may have his own tools, but since you're paying, you reason he should work *your* equipment instead. Especially since you've got a nice big tip waiting for him …

Welcome to the world of *Hired Hands*. Featuring yarns from gay erotica's most prolific tale spinners, this collection is for anyone who's ever lusted after a day laborer or by-the-hour specialist, fantasizing about their above-and-beyond customer service skills. Sometimes the hookups are completely random—as with Sebastian, who visits his mother and winds up in bed with her hot gardener in Jeffrey Hartinger's "A Few Days in Los Angeles." Ditto for Vince, a finely architectured specimen hired to pose for an art school who spends the class break in a men's room stall with an appreciative drawing student in Mike Hicks's "Model Behavior."

And Joe, a window washer who happens to glimpse a hot tryst in progress on the thirty-second story and ends up joining the action in Michael Bracken's "High-Rise Hook-Up."

In other cases, the hired hand answers a desperate call—like the hot mechanic who responds to a stranded driver on a frigid weekend and revs up more than the car in Gregory L. Norris's "Jump-Start." And the impressively-equipped pizza delivery guy who offers up a delicious feast beyond pepperoni to the straight guy who wants to eat naughtily while his wife's out of town. And other times, the fun is the result of a ploy. Such is the case with the private dick who's hired to expose a two-timing scandal and ends up exposing a whole lot more in Landon Dixon's "More Than Meets the Eye" and the hunky house cleaner who angles for additional work—along with some play—in P.A. Friday's "Clean House, Dirty Mind."

A few of the stories show us what happens when disaster turns delicious. Witness the neglected morsel of a canceled event that proves to be a delectable mistake in Rob Rosen's "Top Chef Bottoms" and the unaccompanied mover who ends up singlehandedly tackling a big load with dexterity and aplomb in J.R. Haney's "Moving Out with a Bang." This proves also to be true for Jordan, a new homeowner who finds himself with a bird problem and a pining ache for the animal control specialist he hires in Ryan Field's "Woody's Woodpecker," and Kevin, a young, bored, sexually frustrated jock with a broken leg who ends up getting *all* his needs taken care of by T. Hitman's "Dude Friday."

And then there are those jack-of-all-trades who lend a hand to those who may not even be aware of what they need. Like Abel, the handsome handyman who brings young Jack out of his shell in Abner Ray's "Willing and Abel," and Kyle, a studly rubbish remover who finds himself unable to part with a compulsive hoarder in David Aprys's "College Hunks Haul Junk."

I hope you enjoy these stories and are inspired by them the next time that stud comes to repair your air conditioner or clean your pool. After all, why should you take matters into your own hands when you've got a hunky hired hand?

Winston Gieseke
Berlin

HIGH-RISE HOOK-UP
Michael Bracken

Joe Nelson sat in a bosun's chair thirty-two stories above the street, cleaning the windows of a high-rise condominium. Using a figure-eight motion, he slid a soapy brush over the glass pane before him. Then he repeated the motion with a squeegee, flicked soapy water from the squeegee, and moved to the next window. Two sixty-pound ropes attached to permanent tiebacks on the roof prevented him from plummeting to his death. The main rope was attached to the bosun's chair upon which he sat and the other rope was affixed to the safety harness strapped around his torso. In addition to the brush and the squeegee, hanging from the bosun's chair or from his utility belt were a ten-gallon bucket filled with soapy water, a spray bottle of cleaning solution, and a scraper to clear away bird shit and other sticky substances.

As he moved from window to window, Joe used a single suction cup grabber to stabilize himself. Sometimes the sound of the suction cup thudding against the window startled people on the other side of the glass, but for the most part the condominium's residents ignored the window washer's presence outside their window, just as the people working inside office buildings did. For that reason, he often saw things he should not have seen, from people fast asleep at their desks in the middle of the workday to others in various stages of undress moving about in the false privacy of their homes. Joe usually ignored what he saw because the Peeping Tom aspect of his job wasn't what had drawn him to window cleaning—he had been attracted by the significant increase in pay from his previous position as a janitor—but sometimes he couldn't help himself.

Joe had just finished cleaning someone's living room window and had swung into position to clean the next window when he found himself staring into a bedroom where two naked men were enjoying the pleasure of one another's company. Neither seemed aware of his presence and neither reacted to the thud of his suction cup against the glass. Perhaps because they were in the bedroom of a condominium unit that cost more than he would earn in his lifetime, Joe suspected they were gentlemen he would never encounter in the blue-collar bars where he spent his off hours cruising for companionship.

The slender, dark-haired younger of the two men knelt on the plush carpet with his back to the window and with the older man's cock in his mouth. The older man's black hair had gone gray at the temples and he had the thickset build of someone who spent much of his time sitting behind a desk. Though the older man faced Joe, his eyes were closed and he had his thick fingers wrapped around the back of the younger man's head. He thrust his hips forward and back, pistoning his cock in and out of the other man's mouth.

Joe knew he should wash the window and move on but he hesitated. As he watched the two men, his cock grew rigid, and he became increasingly uncomfortable because the safety harness was not compatible with tight blue jeans and a hard-on. The tempo of the older man's hips increased, and Joe could tell from the look on his face that he was about to cum. The window washer wanted to pull his cock out of his pants and cum with the older man but there was no way that would happen while he was hanging thirty-two stories above the street. Instead, he just watched until the older man slammed his hips against the younger man's face one last time and his entire body tensed with orgasm.

A moment later the older man opened his eyes, pulled his softening cock from the other man's mouth, and saw Joe hanging outside the window. Joe immediately splashed soapy water on the glass and made an incomplete figure eight with his brush. As he squeegeed off the soapy water, the younger man moved to cover himself and the older man crossed the room to stand naked only inches from the window. His thick, saliva-slickened cock hung between his thighs, a thin string of cum briefly swinging from the tip.

He stared into Joe's eyes for a moment. Then he said something over his shoulder that caused the younger man to reach into the inner breast pocket of one of the suit jackets before joining him at the window. A gold business card case exchanged hands. Then the older man opened it, removed a card, and pressed the face of it flat against the glass with the palm of his hand.

Joe stared at the card until he memorized the man's name, the name of his law firm, and his cell phone number. Then he dropped down to the next set of windows.

When the window washer dropped out of sight, Marcus Wainwright peeled his business card from the glass and turned away from the window. He'd been surprised to see someone watching him face-fuck the young paralegal from his law firm but the surprise had quickly turned to interest when he realized the man watching them had a bulge in his jeans that warranted closer inspection. When he'd stood naked before the window staring into the pale blue eyes of the window washer, he'd recognized that the other man's desire wasn't limited to a little blood rushing to his crotch. The man hanging outside of his bedroom window made Wainwright think of a hunky piñata that needed to be whacked off until it erupted with cum.

He'd made the paralegal fetch his business card case because he wanted the man outside to know the interest was mutual. He didn't know if the window washer would call, but he would certainly be the subject of Wainwright's erotic fantasies for some time to come. Thinking about being watched and imagining having his way with the muscular window washer gave him another erection, and he wanted to finish what had been interrupted. He said as much to the younger man as he replaced his business card in the gold case and tossed the case on the bed.

The paralegal pulled the curtains closed and then crossed the darkened room to the nightstand. From it he took a partially used tube of lube, squeezed a dollop into the palm of his hand, and wrapped his hand around Wainwright's stiff cock. He stroked his fist up and down the thick shaft until he had completely covered it with lube. He squeezed another dollop onto his fingertips, lifted his ball sac with his other hand, and coated his ass crack and anal opening with lube.

The paralegal turned and bent over the bed, supporting himself with his hands. Wainwright stepped up behind him and nestled his cock in the younger man's lube-slickened ass crack. He slid his cock up and down several times before he drew back and repositioned himself. He pressed the spongy soft head of his cock against the paralegal's asshole and slowly pressed forward until the younger man opened to him.

14

After he eased his entire length into the paralegal, he drew back until just the head of his cock remained. Then he thrust forward and drew back with a steadily increasing rhythm. Wainwright grabbed the younger man's hips and fucked him hard and fast.

As the younger man accepted each of Wainwright's powerful thrusts, his own cock lengthened, stiffened, and strained with desire. He did nothing about it, and Wainwright continued pumping into his ass until he could no longer restrain himself. He slammed his hips against the younger man's buttocks one last time and then came. He fired a thick wad of warm spunk deep into the paralegal's ass, and they stood locked together until Wainwright's cock quit spasming and began to soften.

He stepped backward, withdrawing from the other man. When the paralegal straightened and turned, Wainwright ignored the younger man's erection and said, "We'd better hurry, or we'll be late to the deposition."

Joe worked his way to the ground one window at a time. As soon as his feet hit the sidewalk, he took his cell phone from his pocket and entered the name and phone number he had memorized earlier. Then he returned to the roof with a fresh bucket of soapy water, moved the safety ropes, and again worked his way down the side of the building.

He finished his assigned section of windows shortly before the rest of the crew finished theirs and was waiting when they humped their safety harnesses and cleaning equipment to the company van. During the ride back to the office, they shared what they had seen through the windows that day. Billy had seen six marijuana plants arranged under a grow light, John had watched a Chihuahua take a dump on someone's Persian Rug, and Carlos had watched a topless blonde vacuum her living room. The other guys peppered Carlos with questions about the blonde and never got around to asking Joe anything.

Watching one man perform a blow job on another had been the highlight of Joe's day. Just thinking about what he had seen made Joe's cock stir inside his jeans. He was so horny that after clocking out, he drove straight to Woody's, a hole-in-the-wall that had been catering to blue-collar men of his predilections since long before students from the nearby university discovered the place. Once inside, Joe straddled a stool at the bar, ordered a beer, and turned to scan the room while he drank. A dozen men like Joe, hired hands and blue-collar workers winding down at the end of the workday, had taken control of the darkened booths that lined two walls, and many of them already had a young companion. Students—alone and in twos and threes—sat at the tables arranged in the center of the room between the booths.

Joe had emptied his beer bottle when he caught the eye of a young man sitting alone at one of the tables nursing his own beer. He was drinking the same brand as the window washer, so Joe had the bartender open two bottles and he carried them to the table where the young man sat. He straddled an empty chair and slid one of the bottles across the table.

"Thanks," the young man said as he took a sip. "I haven't seen you before."

"I've been around," Joe said.

The young man asked what Joe did for a living and Joe told him he washed windows. The young man didn't seem impressed, so Joe added, "On the outside of skyscrapers."

The additional information piqued the young man's interest. "You must not be afraid of heights."

"As long as I'm careful, there's no reason to be afraid." Joe watched the young man's eyes to see if he caught the underlying message. When he felt certain that the young man had, he asked, "And you?"

"Law school. Second year."

"What a coincidence," Joe said. "I saw a couple of lawyers today who were getting into each other's briefs."

"Saw?"

Joe told him exactly what he'd watched while hanging outside the bedroom window. He knew his story aroused his young companion because the law student reached into his lap and adjusted the crotch of his pants.

"You must see a lot of things like that."

"Not as much as you'd think."

They talked for a few more minutes, during which they exchanged first names, before Joe excused himself to use the men's room. Just as he expected, Charles followed.

The window washer locked the door and unbuckled his belt. Then Charles pushed his hands aside, unbuttoned Joe's jeans, and slid down the zipper. He hooked his thumbs in the waistband of Joe's boxer briefs and tugged his briefs and his jeans down as he dropped to his knees.

Joe's cock had remained semi-erect ever since he completed his story about watching the two men in the condominium bedroom, and it pointed at Charles's face. Charles wrapped one hand around the thick shaft and pulled Joe's foreskin away from his cock head. Then he took half of Joe's cock into his mouth and drew back until the swollen glans caught against the back of his teeth.

Charles removed his fist from Joe's cock and pressed his face forward until he had the entire length of the window washer's cock in his mouth. He reached around and grabbed Joe's ass cheeks, his fingernails digging into Joe's skin as he bobbed his head forward and back.

Someone rattled the bathroom door but they ignored it. Whoever it was would have to wait his turn. Joe began pumping his hips in counter-rhythm to the motion of the law student's head, but he wasn't completely in the moment. With his eyes closed, he replayed the condominium bedroom scene against the back of his eyelids. Whether Charles realized it or not, Joe was using the young man as a substitute for the men he'd seen in that bedroom.

When Joe felt his balls tighten and his cock stiffen he knew he would not last much longer. He caught the back of Charles's head in his hands and held it as he thrust his cock deep into Charles's mouth several more times. When he came, he came hard. He fired a thick wad of warm cum against the back of Charles's throat.

Charles swallowed repeatedly and then licked Joe's cock head clean before releasing his oral grip. While Charles pushed himself to his feet, Joe pulled up his pants and tucked himself away. With his stress relieved, Joe figured it was time to head home. When he told the law student that he needed to leave, Charles suggested they swap cell phone numbers.

The paralegal was a trifle with which Wainwright killed time, not someone with whom he felt any real connection. Young lawyers, paralegals, and law clerks were easy enough conquests because they often threw themselves at him in failed attempts to curry his favor. He used each of the sycophants in turn and moved on, fucking his way through the city's legal system like a Viagra-fueled satyr. And he felt unfulfilled.

What he wanted more than anything was a real man, one who did not cower before him or expect *quid pro quo* for their sexual favors. Who better than a man who dangled dozens of stories above the street with nothing but a bit rope to prevent him from certain death?

During the weeks following the window washer's appearance outside his bedroom window, Wainwright rebuffed the advances of three different men he had on his fuck-it list. His desire for sexual release only increased as he denied it of himself, and he wasn't usually one to self-pleasure with so much willing man-meat available. Even so, he found himself doing just that one Friday evening after rejecting yet another potential suitor. He lay naked on his bed with a tube of lube, a box of tissue, and memories of the man hanging outside his bedroom window. With the curtains wide open he could see the city at night and felt reasonably confident no one could see him in his darkened bedroom as he replayed in his mind the moment he'd first noticed the window washer staring through the window.

His cock began to lengthen and stiffen, so he squeezed a bit of lube into the palm of his hand, wrapped his fist around his erection, and stroked himself. As he continued stroking, Wainwright's gaze drifted around the room until it settled on the eyebolt the previous owner had installed in the bedroom ceiling. He imagined many possible uses for it, including a few that involved the window washer and his safety harness.

When his balls tightened and a bit of pre-cum moistened the tip of his cock, Wainwright grabbed a wad of tissue. Just in time, he covered his cock head and caught the thick wad of spunk that shot out.

After a difficult day during which he had been attacked by an aggressive falcon nesting on the sill of a forty-third-floor window, Joe dialed Charles's phone number. The law student answered on the third ring and they made arrangements to meet later that evening.

They didn't spend much time on preliminaries and were in Joe's bedroom less than ten minutes after Charles's arrival. The young man stripped first, leaving his clothes in a heap on the floor. He carried a bit of extra weight, had no tan, and had no visible hair below his neck.

Unlike his young companion, Joe had well-developed arms, shoulders, and chest from repeatedly maneuvering up, down, and across the face of skyscrapers throughout the city, and he made little effort to groom his limited body hair.

By the time the window washer had removed his clothing, both of their cocks stood erect. Charles stepped forward and took Joe's erection in his hand. He stroked his fist up and down the turgid shaft several times before he asked, "You have any lube?"

"On the headboard," Joe said, "next to the magazines."

Charles turned toward the bed, said nothing about the stack of pornographic magazines he found there, and turned back toward Joe with the nearly empty tube of lube in his hand. Joe took it from the law student, applied some to his erection and then, when Charles turned to face away from Joe, to the young man's ass crack.

Joe massaged a glob of lube into Charles's sphincter, feeling his asshole open as Charles relaxed. Joe eased one finger into him, and after a few moments eased in a second finger. Then he removed his fingers and pressed the head of his cock against Charles's anal opening. Joe grabbed his hips and thrust forward, driving his cock deep inside the young man. He drew back and did it again.

Joe pounded into Charles again and again and soon could not stop himself. With one last powerful thrust, he buried his cock inside the young law student and filled his ass with warm spunk. As he held the young man's ass tight against his crotch, he reached around and took Charles's cock in his fist. While he was still spasming within Charles, he fist-fucked the law student.

When Charles came and his cock spewed cum over Joe's fist, his sphincter spasmed around Joe's semi-hard cock, almost as if milking the last drops of cum from Joe. After Charles's sphincter stopped spasming, Joe slowly withdrew his cock and then collapsed on the bed. Charles joined him.

"Why do you do it?" Charles asked. "Why do you wash windows on skyscrapers?"

"After high school I worked for a janitorial service," Joe explained. "One day I was staring out the window when a guy rappelled down from the floor above and cleaned the window in front of me. Later, when I found out how much the job paid and that we were part of the same union, I started asking around."

"You don't do it for the thrill?"

"Thrill?" Joe asked. "It isn't mountain climbing, it's a job. The first time I dropped over the side of a building, I almost shit my pants."

Wainwright didn't answer his cell phone because he was in a meeting with a client and didn't recognize the number when he glanced at the caller ID. Later he listened to the message and heard an unfamiliar voice say, "I'll be washing the windows on your side of the condo tomorrow."

Several weeks had passed since his encounter with the window washer and his desire had only increased. He had his paralegal reschedule the next day's afternoon meetings.

Wainwright had just unlocked his front door when his cell phone announced an incoming text. Believing the message to be from a client or from his office, the attorney didn't check his phone until he reached his bedroom and peeled off his suit coat. When he did, the phone's screen filled with the image of Joe's thick cock and heavy ball sac dangling from a nest of sandy blond pubic hair. Wainwright's cock twitched with desire.

By the time Joe swung into view and his suction cup grabber thudded against the window, Wainwright had shed his clothes.

He crossed the room to the window as he had the first time he'd spotted Joe outside his bedroom, and he stood before the glass with his semi-erect cock grasped firmly in his right hand.

He knew what caused the bulge in the window washer's tight-fitting jeans because he'd had time to appreciate the selfie before Joe's arrival. As Wainwright watched the window washer's eyes, the window washer watched him stroke himself. His cock didn't need much encouragement before it stood at attention. When it did, Wainwright released his grip and pressed his erection against the cool glass, rubbing it against the smooth surface as he pumped his hips up and down.

As Wainwright watched, Joe touched the other side of the glass near his ball sac, ran his finger up the length of Wainwright's cock, and then licked his lips. Wainwright stepped back, wrapped his fist around his cock again, and pumped hard and fast. When he came, he fired a thick wad of spunk that would have struck the window washer's face if glass had not separated them.

Joe watched the spunk slowly crawl down the window. He slid his soapy brush in a quick figure eight on the other side, repeated the motion with his squeegee, and flicked away the soapy water. Then he dropped down to the next set of windows and worked his way to the ground. He wasn't surprised to find the lawyer waiting for him when he reached the sidewalk.

"You put on quite a show, Mr. Wainwright," Joe said as he unfastened himself from the bosun's chair.

"Marcus," the attorney said. "Call me Marcus."

"So, what can I do for you, Marcus?"

"How about drinks at my place Saturday evening?"

"Nothing fancy," Joe said. He named his beer and they agreed on a time.

Wainwright started to walk away and then he turned back.

"Yes?" Joe asked.

"And bring your harness."

Joe arrived at Wainwright's condominium with his safety harness slung over his shoulder and was ushered into the living room where Wainwright had an ice bucket chilling three bottles of Joe's favorite beer. Wainwright had already opened on a bottle of wine for himself, and he poured himself a second glass while Joe put his gear on the floor and opened a beer.

Joe took his drink to the window and stared out at the city for a moment. Then he turned to his host. "Nice view," he said. "I never get to see it like this."

"You must see things other people never see." Wainwright said as he stepped up beside his guest.

"I usually see things I can't have," Joe said.

Wainwright rested his hand on Joe's arm, the first time the two men had any kind of physical contact. "I think that'll change soon."

They stared into each other's eyes for a moment, the first time they'd done that without a thick sheet of glass separating them. Wainwright reached up, ran the back of his hand along Joe's jawline, and then caught the back of Joe's head in his palm. Then Wainwright pressed his lips against Joe's.

The kiss lasted only a moment but sent fire to their loins. They set aside their unfinished drinks and came together a second time, this kiss even deeper. Their tongues entwined, each fighting for dominance.

They both knew why Wainwright had invited Joe to his apartment. Wainwright had dealt with his desire by avoiding carnal contact with other men while Joe had dealt with his desire by fucking a young law student. The time had come to discover if their mutual desire survived the transition from fantasy to reality.

They peeled off one another's clothing, leaving it strewn around the living room and down the hall as they moved into the bedroom, each still attempting to establish dominance over the other until Joe had the attorney pressed flat against the bedroom window and stood with his erect cock nestled in Wainwright's ass crack.

"This why you showed me your card that day?" Joe whispered in the attorney's ear as he slowly pumped his hips forward and back.

"God, yes," Wainwright breathed huskily.

"Why the harness?"

The attorney pointed over his shoulder toward the ceiling and Joe glanced in that direction. He hadn't noticed the eyebolt when he'd watched Wainwright and the other man going at it several weeks earlier, nor when he'd watched Wainwright masturbate for him only a few days earlier, but he knew as soon as he saw it why Wainwright had insisted that he bring his safety harness.

"You sure it'll hold someone?"

"It'll hold at least 500 pounds," Wainwright said. "That's what the previous owner said. I've never tested it."

Joe had never had sex while hanging from his safety harness nor had he ever had sex with someone else hanging from a safety harness. He had never even considered it, but the idea intrigued him. He stepped back, removing his cock from the attorney's ass crack and allowing Wainwright to step away from the glass.

The window washer walked to the living room, returned with his safety harness, and strapped Wainwright into it. Then he stood on a chair to hook the harness to the eyebolt in the ceiling and lifted the attorney off of his feet.

Joe moved the chair aside and turned back. Wainwright was

slowly spinning in a circle, unable to stop himself. Joe grabbed the harness and reached between Wainwright's thighs. He grabbed the man's scrotum and kneaded the attorney's nuts as he stroked the sensitive spot behind the man's sac, almost, but not quite, touching the attorney's anal opening.

"Stop teasing me," Wainwright said. "The lube's in the night-stand."

Joe crossed the room and retuned with a new tube. He slathered his cock with the slick substance and then spun Wainwright around and pushed him forward until the attorney was horizontal, like a skydiver before pulling his chute open. Wainwright waved his arms, swimming in mid-air to keep from turning upside down.

Joe grabbed Wainwright's legs and spread them as he stepped between the attorney's thighs. He coated Wainwright's ass crack with a thick glob of lube and then teased his anal opening with the tip of one finger.

Wainwright's ass slowly opened to Joe's digital probing. Joe slid his finger in and out of the other man several times before he eased in a second finger. When he felt certain the attorney was relaxed enough to take his entire length, Joe withdrew his fingers and pressed the swollen head of his cock against Wainwright's sphincter. He grabbed the attorney's hips and pulled him backward until the attorney was impaled on his stiff cock.

Using the pendulum motion of the safety harness, he pushed the attorney forward and pulled him back, quickly finding a rhythm that both men found enjoyable.

Wainwright was at the window washer's mercy and Joe knew it. He increased the speed of the swinging motion, pushing and pulling the attorney faster and faster until he felt his scrotum tighten and his cock stiffen, and he couldn't restrain himself. He pulled Wainwright's ass tight against him and fired a thick wad of warm spunk deep inside the attorney as Wainwright hooked his ankles together behind Joe's back.

He reached around the attorney and grabbed hold of his erection. He still had a little lube on his hand and he quickly fist fucked the hanging man, driving him toward a quick release that had the attorney firing his wad over the plush carpet.

As the attorney came, his sphincter spasmed around Joe's cock, milking the last of his cum until Joe pushed the man away and stepped aside.

As Wainwright swung back and forth, he asked, "How do I get out of this thing?"

"You don't," Joe told him. "Not until I'm done with you."

Joe stepped out of the bedroom and returned with a fresh beer and Wainwright's unfinished glass of wine. He stopped the attorney, helped him straighten up, and handed him his drink.

They fucked, they drank, and they fucked more.

Half the night disappeared before they exhausted themselves and Joe released the attorney from the safety harness.

When Joe finally left Wainwright's place, his harness in hand, he knew he would never see his job the same way again.

And Wainwright planned to stop fucking his way through the legal system and spend more time with hard-working men who knew exactly how to work him.

MODEL BEHAVIOR

Mike Hicks

Because I was running late, I skipped my usual pre-class cigarette. I shoved my underwear into the locker with the rest of my clothes, donned my terrycloth robe and flip-flops, and headed down to the assignment desk. Cindy gave me a slip of paper with the room number and instructor on it: Ms. Ramirez, Life Drawing 1-B, studio 207. I didn't recognize the name.

Modeling for art classes is about the easiest way there is to make extra cash. All you gotta do is sit or stand there bare-assed for a couple hours in front of a room full of young artists, then you get eighty bucks and you go home. Of course, you have to have one of the kinds of bodies they want. Like mine. The art profs like me for my ultra-defined musculature as much as for my talent for staying really still for a long time. So, I pretty much get all the bookings I want. The extra cash pads out my vacation fund—but honestly, I sometimes think I'd do it for free. Yeah, I've got an exhibitionist streak. Sue me.

Studio 207 was already full of students warming up at their easels when I walked in. Ms. Ramirez turned out to be a chubby no-nonsense type, clearly miffed at my being five minutes late.

"You're here." She smiled tersely. "Please, let's get started." She motioned me toward a two-foot-high platform with a stool on it in the middle of the room. "Your name?"

"Vince." I climbed up on it.

She turned to address the kids. "Class, our model is Vincent. I'd like him to begin in a seated position for an hour, then we'll have a break and come back for a second pose."

She looked to me and nodded. I undid the belt and let the robe slip off my shoulders to the ground. Ms. Ramirez let out an audible gasp, as did a couple of her students. This sometimes happens on my first time with a new class. I should've mentioned that I've got a big cock. It's nearly eight inches even when totally flaccid, or longer if you count the foreskin that covers the tip and hangs down like a bit of fleshy chewing gum. It gets a couple inches longer when erect, but that's usually not an issue when I'm modeling. Back in high school the assholes used to call me "pony boy" in the showers, which embarrassed me only about as long as it took me to figure out the distinct advantages of being horse-hung and how to play them.

There's not really a way to prepare a new class for the first peek. But they get used to it.

I took a seat on the stool, resting my heels on one of the metal rungs with my legs spread wide. The cold metal against my balls made them draw up slightly on contact. I picked up my dick by the head and moved it to a comfortable position, then crossed my arms over my chest. That was the pose. I surveyed the class. A few moments of silence was interrupted by the subtle scratching of charcoal and pencil against paper.

You gotta find ways to kill time while you're sitting there motionless—plan the weekend, mentally pay the bills. Or you can make a game out of it like I do. My favorite pastime is to guess which of the guys are gay and see if I can catch them staring at me inappropriately. My first catch of the evening was a seriously hot goateed little guy. Even from the corner of my eye I could tell his gaze was directed right at my prick. I let him look for a few minutes then busted him with a glance. He blushed so red I almost felt sorry for him.

I let my eyes wander the classroom in search of my next victim. That's when I spotted him. His easel was way back in the corner against the wall. I've never felt so suddenly in danger of an erection. Picture Michelangelo's *David* but made out of luscious pink flesh, the curly hair black instead of ivory. His dark nipples showed through a thin white T-shirt that in general did more to emphasize his body than hide it. I couldn't tell much about the legs under his baggy cargos. He couldn't have been much over twenty, but there was a cocky confidence about him that you usually find only in more mature men—an attitude obvious at a glance, as that kind of confidence always is. His sexual orientation was clear from the way he stared, but the difference between him and any other guy I'd ever played this with was that he didn't look away when I caught him. He fixed his gaze right back on mine. He took his pencil from the paper and let his hand hang to his side—whether he knew it or not, striking a pose that matched that Florentine statue he so closely resembled—then he shifted his eyes down to my crotch. I felt suddenly, oddly, naked. He locked eyes with me and nodded before beginning to sketch again. I smiled. He didn't smile back. I was the one who had to look away.

The exchange inaugurated some activity in my crotch that I desperately needed not to happen right then, so I abandoned the game for the rest of the session and tried to think about what Ms. Ramirez would look like naked. It worked.

When the hour was up she announced a break, and the classroom began to empty out. I pulled my robe back on. A hand on my elbow caught me at the door. I looked back to see Michelangelo's *David* holding a rolled-up sheet of newsprint.

"Hi," I said.

"Thought you might like this," he said. He pressed the paper into my hand.

I took it from him without unrolling it, not quite sure what to make of him. "OK. Thanks."

He strolled out the door down the hall without another word. I went back to the models' lounge. I got a cigarette out of my locker and lit up, then kicked back on the beat-up sofa and unrolled the paper to see how well he'd captured my likeness.

The butt fell out of my mouth, adding another burn to the ratty couch. It wasn't the way he'd captured my body so perfectly—which he had, down to each separate division of my abdominals—but it was the way he'd drawn my prick: erect. It was pointing up at a forty-five degree angle just like it does when I'm aroused, with the head peeking about halfway out of the stretched foreskin: a huge boner just on the edge of being ridiculous, but, thankfully, not quite. The proportions were perfect. How he got it right, I have no idea.

I chuckled when I saw how he'd signed it down in the lower left corner—turned out his name really *was* David. And he'd written what looked to be a phone number beneath it. I grabbed my cell out of the locker and punched in the number. He picked up on the first buzz.

"David?" I asked.

"Yeah."

"This is Vince ... the model."

"I know."

"I wanted to thank you for ..."

He cut me off. "I'm in the third floor men's room. Last stall."

Then a click. He was cocky to assume that I'd join him. He was also correct. I made sure the robe was securely closed before I made my dash for the third floor.

The men's room was near the end of the deserted corridor. The door creaked when I opened it and stepped into the dim light. It slammed shut automatically. The room was lit by a single bare bulb hanging over the urinals. The six stalls faced them. When I reached the one on the end, I could see him through the crack seated on the toilet.

"David?" I whispered.

He opened the door slightly and motioned me in. He'd taken his shirt off. His perfect skin took on a glow in the indirect light. His pants were around his ankles and he was stroking a boner a couple inches shorter than mine. In other words, huge.

"Thanks for the drawing. I liked it."

He didn't speak, still didn't smile, but opened his mouth wide and laid his tongue out before me. I undid the belt and opened my robe to show him how close he'd captured my likeness. He didn't hesitate; he took the cock by the base of the shaft and made a couple dry strokes while he scrutinized it, then he closed his eyes and brought his tongue to the head. He licked it like a lollipop. At the touch of his soft lips on the tip the head almost escaped the foreskin. The sensation made it surge, certainly giving him a taste of my pre-cum. He sucked hard to get more. He reached for my hand and placed it on the back of his head, like he wanted me to help him get my big girth down his throat. I applied pressure and was able to get it almost halfway in. There was a pause with loud retching as I tried to go further. I expected him to give up and let his lips slip back up to the head, but he was a persistent cocksucker. He held it in that same place till his gagging finally subsided, then, taking a moment to inhale through his nose, he swallowed me the rest of me, all the way down to within an inch of my pubes. He was only the second or third guy who'd ever been able to get that far down on me. He held it there with his mouth stretched wildly out of proportion, his face reddening, straining to breathe through his nose. He looked up at me, still cocky as hell. I fucked my prick in and out a few times while he grunted approval.

I was already about to blow. Knowing we had only a few minutes and guessing he wanted my load, I picked up the pace. But as soon as I did, he let the whole thing slip out. He looked up at me and let the slimy head slide around on his chin. I got the impression he was thinking something over. Likely whether he'd be able to take me up the ass or not.

He decided to give it a try. He stood, turned around and dropped his pants, then bent over and laid his face down against the top of the toilet tank. You'd have thought Michelangelo had sculpted his ass as well. And you could tell he knew it was hot by the way he wagged it back and forth a couple times. He reached back and spread his cheeks open wide. The crack was smooth but for a small thatch of downy hairs that ringed his butthole like a halo. The little bud was bright pink and almost frighteningly tiny.

"Hey, bud," I said, "I think I might be too big for you …"

He shook his head and reached for my drooling dick head, expertly positioning it against the dainty little bud. "Try it," he said. "I'll tell you if it's too big."

I made a tentative push against it. It opened with surprising ease to admit the swollen head, then closed firmly around it like a vacuum. He didn't yelp when it popped in, so I kept going. I made a mental note of how my prick looked disappearing into that alabaster butt for use in future masturbatory fantasy. He didn't scream till I made it into him halfway. I stopped.

"No!" he panted. "Keep going." I obeyed. He let out little—and then big—grunts of pleasure and pain as I ground it the rest of the way into him and then began the process of pulling out and plunging in in rhythm. The grunts got louder the harder I fucked. I slowed down, but he didn't want that. *"Harder!"* he screamed. "Fuck me *harder* with that friggin' fence post!" He dug his face into the tank. I obliged, which seemed to unleash his capacity to verbalize. "Take me with that goddamn horse-dick, motherfucker! Yeah! Fuckin' breed my ass …"

God, I love dirty talk …

I heard the door open and slam shut. I put my hand over David's mouth to shut him up, which worked. I stuck a middle finger in his mouth and he sucked it like a pacifier.

The footsteps stopped. There was the sound of a fly being unzipped, then the tinkling of piss against porcelain. I slowed the fuck to a gentle rocking, just an inch or so in and out so as not to make much noise but to keep him aware that I was inside him. The peeing stopped and the guy zipped up. Then the sound of footsteps again and the door opening and swinging shut. I pulled my finger from David's mouth.

"Fuck," he whispered angrily.

"What?"

"I hate it when guys don't wash their hands. I mean, he just had them on his dick for Chrissake …"

"Remind me to wash mine," I said and rammed myself back in deep so hard he gasped. That second round of pounding must've hit the bull's-eye of his prostate, because after only four or five deep fucks I could feel his body start to clench up. His shit hole pulsed against my dick, and right at that moment huge gobs of hot splooge shot out of him and onto the toilet rim. White on white. He dug his face into the tank and writhed and murmured till he finished.

I slid my dick out of him with a wet *pop* just in time to blow a thick load. It landed on the small of his back and dripped slowly down into his crack as we both got our breaths. I took a fingerful of my semen and worked my finger between his cheeks. I used it like lotion to soothe his wounded pussy. It clenched and loosened rhythmically with my touch.

I pulled on my robe and went over to the sink to wash my hands, while he wiped his DNA off the toilet. I looked back over my shoulder to make sure he'd made note of my good hygiene. A quick check of my watch indicated the fifteen-minute break had ended five minutes earlier. *Fuck.* I turned go. "That was amazing, David," I said.

He nodded but didn't smile. "Yeah, it was. Thanks." He flushed a wad of toilet paper soggy with our sperm.

"See you back in class."

I jogged down a floor and into room 207 to find the room full of would-be artists waiting impatiently at their easels. Ms. Ramirez saw me, looked at her watch, and rolled her eyes.

"Sorry I'm late," I said. "Had to, uh … wash my hands."

David sauntered leisurely into the studio and took his place in the far corner. I climbed up on the platform and dropped the robe for the third time that night. Ms. Ramirez let out a small shriek. I looked down and saw the problem: I was still semi-erect. I blushed and tried to fold my hands over it, which didn't work very well. I told you it's big.

She cleared her throat. "Vincent," she said. "I'd like you to do a prone pose for the second session. Think you can manage that?"

"Sure, Ms. Ramirez." I laid the open robe on the platform, then lay down on it on my stomach. I propped myself up on my elbows and surveyed the room until I spotted David. We locked eyes again. He still didn't look away. But for the first time his lips were curled into something that resembled a smile.

34

WOODY'S WOODPECKER
Ryan Field

When Jordan bought a summer home in the hills of north eastern Pennsylvania, he knew there would be a few structural and
cosmetic issues. He'd planned ahead financially to deal with them
because he'd paid less for the house than he'd expected. He also
knew he would have to hire people.

Coming from Brooklyn, New York, where he worked as a high
school teacher and lived in a small condo in Brooklyn Heights, his
tool box consisted of a butter knife and Scotch tape. To make matters even more complicated, he'd purchased his small cabin near
the Delaware Water Gap in the dead of winter—without seeing
everything the way it would look in the spring when all the snow
had melted. In the future, he would warn everyone he knew to
never buy a house when there's a foot of snow on the ground.

On the first relatively warm weekend in April, weeks before
most of the trees and shrubs would bloom in full, Jordan drove west
to Pennsylvania early on a Saturday morning. Although the cabin
was only a one-thousand-square-foot cedar and stone A-frame ski
lodge built in the mid-1970s, it had a well, a septic system, and

electric baseboard heat. There was also a wood-burning stove in the main living space that the realtor promised him would heat the entire place. So Jordan wasn't worried about the fact that the temperature that sunny April morning hadn't risen above fifty degrees. He'd even stopped at a corner market in Brooklyn to pick up a few groceries and a bundle of firewood just in case.

But when he pulled into the narrow, unpaved driveway that led back to his cabin, the rear wheel of his BMW coupe started to spin in the mud. Unable to go forward, he had to leave the car parked sideways and walk the rest of the way to the cabin. He noticed that what had once been a gravel driveway had been neglected and now needed a top layer of fresh gravel. He hadn't seen this when he'd looked at the house two months earlier with all the snow.

By the time he reached the house, his new Gucci half boots were covered in mud. He climbed two rickety wooden steps that led to a large lopsided deck in front of the house and set his bag of groceries on a built-in bench with rotted boards. Checking his pockets for keys, he glanced around at the warped deck and frowned. Several of the planks had separated from the foundation and were sticking up. Others had been removed and never replaced. The deck had also been covered with snow the last time he'd been there. He'd seen the photos the previous owners had taken, but he realized now that those photos had probably been taken twenty years ago.

When he finally found his keys, he loped to the front door, unlocked it, and forced it open with his shoulder after a more gentle approach failed. His first mission was to remove the Gucci boots and clean them, and as he gently rubbed the mud off, he glanced around at the interior and remembered why he'd purchased this cottage instead of others he'd seen. The floors were solid wide planks of pumpkin pine, the ceiling a two-story affair with wooden beams that crossed and arched, and on both sides of the main living space there were two walls of solid stone. The front wall was mostly glass. He remembered feeling as if he'd stepped into an old bank house from the 1700s the first time he'd entered.

Though he later managed to get the BMW out of the mud and up next to the house, there were a few more challenges that first weekend. The neat little wood package he'd bought in Brooklyn lasted all of twenty minutes in the wood burning stove and the shower head broke off in his hand when he tried to adjust it. On top of that, two out of four burners on the thirty-year-old electric range in the kitchen refused to heat up. Though he'd been overwhelmed at first, wondering how he could have been so careless buying a place that needed this much work, by Sunday afternoon he frowned as he packed the car to head back to Brooklyn.

The weekends that followed were spent lining up the most needed renovations. First, he ordered new gravel for the driveway, and then he hired a contractor to completely rebuild the deck in front of the house. When June rolled around, he didn't even wait until the weekend to leave Brooklyn. He packed everything he'd need for a few months, climbed into his BMW, and headed west without so much as a backward glance. He was twenty-nine years old and this was the first vacation he'd taken in seven years. He'd taken day trips to the Hamptons with friends. He'd taken weekend trips to Provincetown. But he hadn't been out of New York for more than a long weekend since college. He'd also reached that point in his life where meeting the right man wasn't his main concern anymore. He'd dated more men than he could count. He'd slept with more men than he was willing to admit. So far, the right "one" had not come along and he was tired of putting his life on hold. Buying this cabin was the first thing he'd done for himself in ages.

The first week he spent doing little things around the house and shopping for a few basic pieces of furniture. By the beginning of

July he felt as if he'd settled into a routine and everything seemed less daunting than it had the month before. If it hadn't been for that damn pecking noise he began hearing the second week of July, life would have been perfect.

It started early one morning as he was lying in bed naked with one hand on his dick and the other between his legs. He hadn't met any men he'd wanted to sleep with yet and he had urges that wouldn't go away on their own. He lifted his legs higher, shoved two fingers into his ass, and started tugging on his cock. But just when he was about to imagine James Franco fucking him bareback over the back of a leather chair, this odd pecking sound came from the wall above his bed.

He ignored the sound until the imaginary James Franco came in his ass and he came all over his chest. As he stood up to take a shower, he punched the wall above his bed and the pecking noise stopped. But when he came out of the shower and started to dress, the pecking noise returned and he punched the wall again. Then he went out back and noticed a few unusual chips and cracks in the siding.

In the course of one week the pecking noise continued, the chips and cracks turned into little round holes, and Jordan realized he had a woodpecker problem. When he drove into town to buy supplies to fill the holes, he spoke to a man at the hardware store who told him it was a common problem in the area and some people had to replace their siding every few years because of it. Jordan stood there with a horrified expression and asked, "What can I do to get rid of them?"

The guy in the hardware store laughed and said, "Not much. They're a protected species so you can't kill them. No exterminator will touch a woodpecker job. The best you can do is try to scare them away somehow. I know this guy who used to work for animal control and it's his specialty. If you want, I can give you his number."

"Yes, please," Jordan said. "I'll do whatever it takes."

He dialed the number the second he sat down in the car. He didn't want to do anything illegal, and he certainly didn't want to hurt the woodpeckers. But in the same respect he wasn't a millionaire who could replace siding every two years. As it was, he could barely afford the things he'd already done on a high school teacher's salary. He left a message on the guy's voice mail and drove back to the cabin where he found the beginnings of two new woodpecker holes. He even caught a glance of the woodpecker that had done the damage and tried to frighten him away with the garden hose. He'd never seen a woodpecker until then. It was much smaller than he'd imagined, and nowhere near as intimidating as the holes it made.

About two hours later, a man with a deep throaty voice was on the phone. "I got your message about a woodpecker problem you're having," he said. "I can come out later today and take a look …"

A few minutes before seven that evening, a massive red pickup pulled up to the house. Jordan had been reading a men's fitness magazine on the deck. Although he'd never been fanatical about weight lifting and exercise, Jordan did keep himself in shape. He belonged to a gym in Brooklyn and went three or four times a week. And that summer in Pennsylvania he'd hiked every morning for an hour and done push-ups and sit-ups before showering. At five feet nine inches tall, he was naturally compact, so it wasn't difficult for him to maintain a toned body. Friends often quipped that he reminded them of a young Brad Pitt, except with brown hair so dark it looked black and a more olive complexion thanks to the Italian genes on his mother's side of the family. And while he did trim his body hair, he'd never been one of those men who shaved it all away.

And from the way it looked at a glance, neither did the woodpecker guy. As he unfolded from the pickup, Jordan noticed a thick full beard and mustache with reddish brown highlights. The hair on his head was darker without the red highlights and he wore it short, parted on the side. And when the guy closed the door and stood all the way up, Jordan saw that he was well over six feet four inches tall.

Jordan met him at the front of the truck and extended his right hand. "I'm Jordan Clement. It's nice to meet you."

The guy shook his hand and said, "I'm Woody." He didn't offer a last name. Instead, he glanced up at the house and said, "Nice place."

"Thanks. I'm really hoping you can help. I've been reading up on the Internet about woodpecker problems and I can't seem to find any real solution."

Woody shoved his hands into the pockets of his faded jeans and turned toward the front deck. As he looked up and glanced at the trees, he frowned, rubbed his beard, and said, "It's a real issue, man. I can't tell you how many times I've had to deal with woodpeckers."

"I'll take you around back and show you what they've done so far," Jordan said. "I've already filled in some of the holes with filler, but I just noticed a new one forming this afternoon."

As Jordan turned to lead the way to the back, he noticed the way Woody's tight white T-shirt hugged his chest muscles and biceps. When they reached the back and Woody pulled his hands out of his pockets, Jordan noticed the size of them and almost tripped over a rock. They reminded him of small dinner plates, with thick, long fingers. And the fuzzy reddish brown hair on his forearms matched the color of his beard. Jordan couldn't help wondering if the hair around the big man's dick was the same shade of reddish brown.

They spotted a woodpecker in a tree and Woody went into a short explanation of what he could do to get rid of them. As he spoke about hanging shiny tin pie plates and fake owls that might scare them away, Jordan stood there nodding his head wondering what it would be like to lick Woody's biceps for the next three hours. It had been a long time since he'd met a man that turned him on this much. With each word Woody spoke, Jordan felt something stir in his own pants. With each move Woody made, Jordan imagined what it would be like to be pinned under him. And with each glance Woody gave him, Jordan found it harder to concentrate on woodpeckers.

By the time Woody was finished speaking, Jordan would have done anything to get him to return to the house. Woody said he could start early in the morning. "I can't promise anything, man—I can only do my best."

Jordan nodded. "Understood."

"By the way, I also do other things, too," Woody continued. "I'm a licensed contractor."

Jordan smiled. "That's good to know. There are plenty of things I need done." He even had a few things in mind that didn't include home renovation.

Early the next morning, Jordan heard the sound of a car door slam and sat up in bed. Glancing at a clock on the nightstand, he saw it was a little after six in the morning. During the school year Jordan was usually awake by then, but since he'd been in the cabin he hadn't been waking before nine. This guy wasn't joking when he said he'd be there early in the morning. Jordan then heard a knock on the front door and jumped out of bed fast. He reached for a robe on a chair near the bed, but then changed his mind and grabbed a pair of white boxer briefs instead. He didn't plan on doing anything obnoxious or lewd because he didn't know if Woody was gay. In Woody's case it was hard to tell, which seemed to be happening more often than not to Jordan.

Woody knocked again and Jordan shouted toward the main living space. "I'll be right out." Then he put on the boxer briefs and an oversize white T-shirt. He wanted to look natural, as if he were just walking around the house in his underwear.

When he opened the door, he found Woody standing on the deck smiling. "I hope it's not too early, man. I realize I didn't mention an exact time."

Jordan shrugged and said, "Not a problem. I've been up for hours." He made no reference at all to the fact that he was in underwear. But he did notice that Woody was wearing a tighter pair of jeans that morning, with a large bulge in the crotch, and a tight black T-shirt that pulled across his chest muscles.

Woody smiled warmly. "I'll go around back and get started."

Jordan wanted to jump up, wrap his legs around him, and lick his neck. "Would you like coffee or anything?"

Woody turned and sent him a backhanded wave. "No, I'm good. But thanks."

As he headed toward the stairs, Jordan said, "If you need anything, let me know."

"OK."

An hour later, Jordan walked around back and announced that he was going for his morning hike. There was a trail behind the house that lead to a state park, and it had so many trails that Jordan could do a different hike every morning of the week. Woody was sitting on a small folding stool. He had a butterfly net in one hand and a small cage resting on the grass nearby. He didn't turn or even look up at Jordan, so Jordan went for his hike and left him alone.

This became a pattern that lasted a week and a half. The only difference was that Woody didn't bother knocking on the front door each morning. He just went to the back of the house and waited for the woodpeckers to show up. Jordan would go back and check on him at various times to see if he wanted anything or if he'd caught one. Jordan did this wearing jeans and no shirt one morning, underwear another morning, and even a short bathrobe on several occasions. And he would always receive the same response: Woody would send him a backward glance from the stool and say, "It's all under control."

Unfortunately, Woody didn't catch even one of the pests. And by the middle of the second week, the back of the house looked worse than before. Worse than that, he'd flirted, flaunted, and wiggled his ass enough to deduce that Woody wasn't gay and had stopped trying to get the sexy big man's attention. The only thing he wanted now was to get Woody out of there so he wouldn't go to bed sexually frustrated each night.

He'd find another way to deal with the woodpeckers.

One morning as Jordan was in the bedroom silently rehearsing his "this isn't working" speech, he wandered into the main living space and jumped so fast he knocked over a table. He'd just showered and hadn't dressed yet. His hair was still damp and he hadn't styled it. He'd gone for his hike and had been avoiding Woody all morning. He'd planned to talk to him around lunchtime.

But Woody was standing in the middle of his living room, not far from the front door, gaping at him with a horrified expression. "I'm sorry, man. I didn't mean to scare you. I knocked and no one answered. I got worried and figured I'd come in to check on things."

Jordan grabbed a book from a table and covered his private parts. "I was showering."

"I'm sorry," Woody said. He turned and faced the kitchen wall.

"But you shouldn't leave the door unlocked that way. Anyone could just walk right in."

"Obviously," Jordan said, moving closer to the sofa where he'd left a jacket.

As Jordan put on the jacket, Woody said, "I wanted to talk to you. This woodpecker problem doesn't seem to be getting better. I've done everything I know and they just keep coming back. Which leaves me with only one solution."

Jordan buttoned the jacket and frowned. It was so short if stopped at the bottom of his ass. But at least he wouldn't have to bring this conversation up himself. He felt a wave of relief and said, "What's the solution? You can turn around now. I'm not naked. I'm wearing a jacket. And even if I was naked, what's the big deal? We're just two guys." He tried to keep from having an edge in his tone. But it was hard because he was frustrated that Woody hadn't shown any interest in him. Or solved his woodpecker problem.

Woody turned slowly and looked at him. He lowered his eyes to the floor and said, "I think you should forget about having wood siding back there and do the rest of the house in stone just like the side walls. It'll get rid of the woodpeckers and you'll never have to worry about them doing major damage again. They might try to peck at the trim, but that's only a minor repair compared to siding. I can do the stone work for you and I won't charge much. I think it would look really good, too."

At first, Jordan wanted to throw something at him. But then he thought about how much he loved the stone walls and realized that Woody was right. The back wall and the few small places that weren't glass on the front would look better in stone. And it would probably help insulate the house more, too.

"How much will it cost?" Jordan asked, walking closer.

Woody was still looking down at the floorboards as if terrified to look Jordan in the eye. He shrugged and gave Jordan an off-handed estimate that didn't sound bad at all. Then he said, "And of course I'll give you a huge discount, too. I feel bad about not getting rid of those peckers like I said I would."

Jordan was now right next to him. "It's OK. You told me you couldn't promise anything." By now he wasn't the least bit uncomfortable wearing just a short jacket. In fact, he felt relieved to have been offered a solution that sounded as if it would work. As he turned toward the kitchen and leaned over the counter to pour himself another cup of coffee, he realized the jacket was riding up, exposing half of his naked ass. "Would you like some?" he asked, meaning coffee.

Woody hesitated, and then said, "I'd *love* some."

But as Jordan reached for another mug, he felt a big hand on his ass. He stopped moving and stood there for a moment without saying a word. He finally cleared his throat and said, "I didn't think you were gay."

Woody's hand went up and down his ass slowly. "I wasn't sure *you* were. It's hard to tell sometimes."

Jordan slowly turned to face him. Woody was wearing another tight white T-shirt that hugged his biceps. Jordan grabbed both biceps and squeezed them gently. "I've been dropping hints all week. What did you think when you saw me walking around in my underwear …?"

"I didn't know what to think," Woody said. "I just went home with blue balls every night."

Jordan smiled and unbuttoned the jacket. He removed it and tossed it on the floor. As Woody grabbed his waist, he reached up and held the big man's shoulders. "I'm so sorry—if only I'd known that, you would have gone home with a big smile on your face each night."

Woody pulled him closer and kissed his neck. "Man, you feel so good." His full beard sent chills all over Jordan's body.

"So do you," Jordan said, as Woody's big hands slid down his back and rested on his ass again.

They didn't talk much after that. They kissed for a minute and then Jordan went down on his knees and unfastened Woody's jeans. As he slowly pulled out the big man's dick, Woody pulled off his T-shirt and threw it on top of the jacket Jordan had been wearing. The man's tool was just as Jordan had imagined: a dick long and thick, with a big round head, and a nice reddish brown patch of pubic hair that matched his beard. Jordan grabbed the hard shaft with one hand and rested his other against Woody's thigh. As he wrapped his lips around the head of Woody's dick and ran his tongue across the bottom slowly, Woody grabbed the back of Jordan's head with one hand and leaned backward a little.

Jordan remained on his knees for so long that morning that he had to shove the jacket and T-shirt beneath them because they were starting to sting. He'd learned how to suck a big, thick dick years ago and he didn't want to waste an inch of Woody's. Each time he sucked Woody to the back of his throat, he felt the man's pubic hair brush against his nose. He would linger there for a second or two while Woody applied gentle force to the back of his head, and then he would slide the cock out of this mouth, suck on the head, and repeat the same thing all over again.

He would have sucked Woody's entire load that morning if Woody hadn't grabbed his head and said, "Let's fuck now."

Woody was looking down at him, his dick still in Jordan's mouth. He sucked gently, looked into Woody's eyes, and nodded in approval, knowing instinctively he would be on the receiving end of that fuck session and Woody would be pecking his hole.

When Woody grabbed his arms and lifted him up, he didn't

resist. When Woody held him tightly and started kissing him, he shoved his tongue into the big man's mouth as deeply as Woody had. They kissed and walked back toward the counter. At first, Jordan wasn't sure where they were going to fuck. He wondered if Woody would drag him to the sofa and turn him over. For a minute or two he had a feeling Woody might throw him down on the floor and fuck him on his back. He didn't care where Woody fucked him and he submitted completely when the big man guided him to the kitchen counter, grabbed his waist, and lifted him up.

They were deep in that erotic zone that only happens once in a while if people are lucky, where they communicated between kisses with nods and glances. When Woody set Jordan down on the counter, Jordan looked into his eyes and nodded. Woody smiled, kissed him, and spread Jordan's legs apart. Though Woody's jeans and underwear were down around his ankles now he still hadn't removed them and Jordan could see he wasn't about to.

Jordan spread his legs wider and said, "You have to wear a condom."

Woody pulled his wallet out of his pants. Then he pulled a pre-lubricated condom out of it and covered his dick, having to stretch and tug the thing in order to cover his massive erection. As he did this, Jordan caressed the back of his neck and ran his fingertips all over his shoulders.

Jordan leaned back against the kitchen cabinet. He lifted his legs up so he could throw them over Woody's fuzzy forearms, and he held Woody's shoulders as Woody leaned over to kiss him again. Their tongues locked and the big man guided the head of his dick into Jordan's body so slowly it sent shocks of pain and pleasure all over Jordan's lower half. The deeper Woody went, the more they kissed. The more they kissed, the faster the pain turned into pleasure.

The counter turned out to be the perfect height, perfectly balanced between Woody's dick and Jordan's ass. By the time Woody started pumping in and out slowly, Jordan's knees were even with his shoulders and his legs were dangling over the big man's forearms. Jordan pointed his toes and threw his head back as Woody fucked him faster. Woody's elbow hit a coffee mug and it crashed to the floor. He started fucking even faster after that, and Jordan braced himself for what he knew would be a climax he'd remember for a long time. Not only had he never been fucked by a man like Woody, he'd never been fucked on a counter in this position. He felt as helpless and overwhelmed as he did special and charmed. He held Woody's shoulders and each time they kissed he made a point of licking Woody's beard.

At one point, Woody looked into his eyes and said, "Oh shit, man. Oh fuck."

Jordan knew he was about to cum. He grabbed Woody's head, nodded, and said, "Yes."

A moment after that, Woody rammed his dick as far into Jordan's ass as he could and went dead still for a second or two. After he came, he looked up and started pumping fast again. Jordan started jacking his own dick and came a few seconds later. He shot so far his cum soared up in an arc and landed on Woody's nose.

Woody blinked. "Damn."

Jordan smiled, grabbed Woody's head, and licked the cum off his nose. They remained this way for a few more minutes, kissing with less obnoxious moves.

Woody was still inside Jordan when they heard a woodpecker at the back of the house. Woody stopped pumping and said, "Should I go out there and see if I can get him?"

Jordan spread his legs wider. "No. You're not finished in here. We're going to take a long hot bath in a few minutes, we're going to talk about the dirty things we're going to do next time, and I'm going to rub every inch of your body ..." Jordan paused, and then said, "Unless you'd rather go outside and worry about woodpecker holes."

Woody pushed deeper and said, "I'd rather worry about *your* hole." Then he patted Jordan's ass and kissed him again.

A FEW DAYS IN LOS ANGELES
Jeffrey Hartinger

Sebastian was slightly alarmed when the elderly lady sitting next to him shook him awake. "Excuse me, honey," she said, her southern drawl thick and twangy. "But do you know what time we're supposed to land? The stewardess hasn't been back this way in a bit."

He looked around—first at the old woman, who was dressed pretty elaborately (even for a flight from New York to Los Angeles) and then at the surrounding passengers, who were either sleeping or had their eyes glued to a screen or magazine in front of them. He could have been upset, but he let out a silent laugh and brushed off his annoyance. Even though it was only for two days, this was still a vacation, and he was going to enjoy himself. He *had* to enjoy himself.

"Uhm ... we should be arriving ..." he trailed off, putting on his thick black glasses and bringing his attention to his watch, "... in about an hour or so, if I'm not mistaken."

"Oh, that's good. OK," she responded. "I just wanted to check. You can go back to sleep, sweetie."

Why, thanks, Sebastian thought, *how considerate of you.* "I actually have to run to the restroom. Excuse me." His round ass was thick and defined, and when he scooted past the older woman, she caught a glimpse and smiled to herself.

At five-foot-six, Sebastian was relatively short, yet stern. His tucked-in button-down shirt revealed his bulging muscles, even with a dark green pullover sweater hugging his upper torso. He had a gorgeous body with a matching face, but he didn't feel the need to flaunt it. His dirty blond hair fell easily above his eyes.

At thirty-four-years-old, Sebastian was west coast chill, but direct and friendly in equal ways after spending a decade in New York City. There were many types of men that he longed for, so he was pretty content with his Los Angeles upbringing as well as the diversity that came with living in one of the largest cities in the world. He was a very attractive man and did well for himself. It didn't hurt that he was sweet, too.

Darker men always appealed to Sebastian. And in a multicultural city like New York, there didn't seem to be a shortage of them. The hairy Italian man who owned the deli a block from his apartment always gave him a hard-on; he'd let his eyes wonder as he waited for his pizza or an unhealthy sub after a fun night out. Abdul, the Middle Eastern driver he'd call when he needed a ride to the airport, had a thick frame that made Sebastian feel even more petite. He always got a massive boner when the driver let his right arm hang casually across the tops of the seats. Sebastian would press down on his cock slowly and moan as Abdul talked in his heavily accented voice.

And then there was the Spaniard who'd recently moved into Sebastian's Hell's Kitchen apartment building. He was gruff, even intimidating, and some nights Sebastian would jerk off fantasizing about being fucked doggy style in the laundry room two floors down. He wasn't into public sex, but it made him cum quickly when he thought about being dominated by such a brute. He was easy-going, but in the bedroom he loved being controlled and bossed around. It brought a smile to his face whenever he imagined a thick set of balls smacking against his perfect ass.

Sebastian made his way to the back of the plane and caught the tail end of a conversation. Two female flight attendants were laughing in hushed tones. Sebastian smirked as he closed the bathroom door. One of his best friends from college had worked in the profession for a few months after graduation. "You wouldn't believe some of the shit I have to deal with," his friend Sue would say when they found time to catch up over the phone. "Some of these people are so disgusting and disrespectful. And the worst part? The worst offenders are usually in business or first class!"

Well, apparently not everyone in first class was an asshole. Sue eventually met a private chef on a late-night flight to London and married less than a year later. Sebastian was optimistic about his own romantic future, but still had anxiety about settling down. Whenever he got down on himself, he would think of Sue and her chance meeting on the plane. Anything was possible, right?

"Sorry, I'm back," Sebastian said to the old woman in the seat next to his. "Could I scoot by again?"

When she didn't answer, he asked again—which caused her to jerk suddenly. "Jesus Christ!" she hissed. "Couldn't you tell I was sleeping …?"

Since it was early in the morning, Sebastian figured the ride to his mother's house near the water in Santa Monica wouldn't take long. He grabbed his small bag and made his way to the taxi stand. Ever since he was a kid, he'd request that the air conditioning be turned off so he could roll the windows down. He loved the California air. The cab drivers seemed impartial, but his friends and family always looked at him like he was crazy.

"Ah, fuck. I should have scheduled an Uber," he muttered to no one in particular as he lugged his bags to the end of the snaking line. The woman in front of him nodded. Sebastian only came into town once or twice a year, but he knew better than to annoy his friends or family with LAX pick-up requests.

While in line, he sent his mother a text message and she responded, even though it was five thirty in the morning. "HApp y to see youhave arrived. Love you i will see you soon," she wrote.

His mother had requested they text more often; she was the last of her friends to learn this new communication method, and like everyone in Los Angeles, she didn't want to feel left out.

Sebastian woke up a few hours later. He splashed some cold water onto his face and then made his way into the kitchen. On the counter next to the coffee machine was a note:

Hi honey. Sorry, I did not want to wake you after a long flight. I should be back around three—Carla had an emergency and needed me to watch Max. Text me if you need me. The cash near the sink is for our yard man. Love you. Enjoy the day. It's supposed to be gorgeous out!

The letter made Sebastian smile. He was happy to be home. And since he was officially on vacation, he did the first thing that came to mind: He plopped down on his favorite couch and turned on the big screen TV that was hooked onto the wall.

"This is the life," he said out loud, even though he was the only one home. "I could get used to this." He powered down his iPhone and tossed it onto the coffee table. One hand went behind his head and the other one into his pants.

Twenty minutes later, he heard a car pull into his mother's

driveway. Peering through the living room curtains, he watched as the truck reversed slightly and a large Hispanic man with a buzz cut stepped out of the car.

Holy shit, Sebastian thought, completely fixated on the handsome dark-skinned man. *Who the fuck is that?*

He felt blood rush to his cock immediately; he was completely hard within ten seconds. Despite having reached his mid-thirties, he'd never had his dick spring to attention so quickly. But the man was the epitome of perfection, so it was hardly a surprise.

Figuring he should see what the man wanted, Sebastian tried to compose himself—which meant flipping his boner into the waistband of his dark blue sweatpants. He wasn't wearing underwear, and even though he was only planning to crack the door slightly, he didn't want an accident to happen.

"Hi, how are you?" Sebastian called from the front door, his voice cracking with anxiety. When the man didn't respond, he called out again.

"Hi there. Can I help you?"

"Oh, me? Sorry, sorry. I'm doing well, bud. I assume you know Ms. Barton?" The man looked a little caught off guard and seemed to Sebastian to be equally anxious.

Sebastian paused a second before responding. He surveyed the man's body, taking in his beautiful details as the overbearing California sun reflected off his frame. He looked to be in his early fifties and was pretty tall, seeming around six-two or six-three in the distance. His curly black hair was slicked back with gel. Although he couldn't see his backside, Sebastian knew the man had a beautiful and muscular ass.

Oh, and how he loved a beautiful, meaty ass.

Nothing turned Sebastian on more than a powerful daddy-type. Which meant a man could be forceful as he drove his dick into Sebastian's mouth or ass. It was one of his favorite things to grab both ass cheeks as he took a man entirely into his mouth.

"Uh, yeah, she's my mom. But she's out for the day. I have a check for you—do you want it now?"

The man smiled at Sebastian and made his way up the driveway. When he was ten feet or so away, he took off his sunglasses and held out his right hand.

"It's nice to meet you, buddy," he said, grabbing onto Sebastian's hand and shaking it firmly for about two seconds. "My name is Carlos."

"Sebastian," was all he could mutter, completely mesmerized by the beautiful Hispanic man in front of him.

They continued to stare at each other for a few seconds—Carlos looking down at Sebastian with a telling smile on his face—as a laugh track from an old sitcom boomed from the living room.

"And, uh, naw, that's fine, brotha. Why don't I grab it before I head out?"

"Uhm ... grab *what* ...?" Sebastian asked nervously, his mind elsewhere.

"The check. For the yard work. I'm only doing minor stuff today—I'll let you know when I'm done. Probably in an hour or so."

"Oh, yeah," Sebastian said awkwardly and a little too loud. "That works."

He watched as Carlos turned and made his way back towards his truck. There was indeed a perfect ass there and Sebastian licked his lips at the sight of it. Carlos had two perfect, muscular globes that were beautifully showcased in his tight dark pants.

After letting out a quiet moan, Sebastian closed the door and made his way to the back of the house to take a shower. He definitely needed to jerk off and cool down.

It was a calm Saturday, and nothing had changed since he'd lived here. A violin was being played somewhere in the neighborhood, and across the backyard he spotted an older Asian man who was quizzing his son on their sprawling back porch. He laughed and reminded himself that he was in the land of rich, overbearing parents and the kids who couldn't wait to go away to school. He was one of them once.

As he jumped in the shower, Rod Stewart blared from his laptop.

Maybe he was still groggy, but he couldn't shake the idea that something was going to happen later that day. Meeting Carlos had only increased the feeling. He didn't want to cum just yet but he yanked at his cock and let a wet finger slide into his tight ass as he fantasized about the hot gardener fucking him senseless.

He dried off and tossed his towel on the bed. Glancing out a side window, he noticed Carlos in the yard. He'd taken his shirt off, and the sweat dripped slowly from his body. His chest was buff and strong, and it looked even better to Sebastian now that it was bare and on display. The thick hair covering the man's body turned him on further still, and Sebastian's breathing began to get heavy. Instinctively, Sebastian grabbed for his cock and slowly backed himself onto the bed. He was really getting into it when he heard a knock at the front door.

"Ah, shit," he said as he jumped up and ran into the bathroom. He grabbed his old high school robe from behind the door and made his way down the hall. Just before he opened the door, he made sure the robe was wrapped around him and tied securely.

"Hey! Sorry about that. I was just taking a shower ... I always feel dirty after traveling ... but I passed out right when I got home from the airport. Do you want to come in?" Sebastian was stammering, something he always did when he was nervous or liked someone.

Carlos grinned. "Yeah, can I grab something to drink, bud?" His shirt, still off, was tossed casually over his right shoulder. His musk was overwhelming, but in a good way. Carlos smelled good—like a man who had spent the day working in the sun.

"Sure," Sebastian replied, turning and walking toward the kitchen, Carlos just behind him. "What would you like? Is water or lemonade OK?"

"Water works just fine. Thanks, buddy."

Sebastian grabbed a water bottle from the fridge and tossed it across the room. Carlos caught it, popped open the cap and downed the contents in a few seconds.

"Ah," he breathed. "I needed that. Thanks, son."

"No problem," Sebastian responded.

Carlos was looking at him strangely, a lopsided grin on his face.

"What?" Sebastian asked, sounding more paranoid than he'd intended.

Carlos motioned his eyes towards Sebastian's crotch, where his robe was slightly parted to the side, exposing his massive boner. Sebastian instantly turned red and turned away from Carlos to close the robe.

"I'm sorry. I, uh … it must be the robe. It's not you. I'm so sorry." Sebastian said, more anxious than ever, and realizing how stupid he sounded.

"Not me? Damn. I went ahead and flattered myself, buddy. I guess this old guy just doesn't have it anymore."

Sebastian turned around slowly and looked at Carlos. The look of lust was evident in his eyes—staring Sebastian down from across the kitchen, he licked his lips.

"Drop the robe, boy," Carlos said after a second, authoritative but still gentle. "Let me see that beautiful bubble butt of yours— I've been thinking about bending you over from the second I laid eyes on you." Sebastian cautiously dropped the robe. Carlos made a twirling motion with his right index finger. "Turn around. Let me see that white boy ass."

Sebastian turned, arching his ass towards Carlos and putting one hand against the fridge. Carlos made his way across the room and whispered into his ear, rubbing the growing bulge in his pants against Sebastian's bare ass.

"You gonna be my little bitch, boy? Huh? You come all the way back home to please your daddy?"

"Yes, sir," Sebastian moaned, turning around so he could be face-to-face with Carlos. Only inches apart, Sebastian noticed the handsome gardener had beautiful brown eyes with a hint of green. The hair on his face was completely black, expect for a few white whiskers sprinkled in.

Carlos took Sebastian in his arms and brought their lips together—pausing for a second to let their breathing slow to a consistent and collective moan—and then they began to kiss. As Sebastian brought his hand to Carlos's hard, throbbing bulge, he felt two or three fingers begin to play around his asshole. He moaned louder. Carlos didn't flinch.

"Let's go to the bedroom, boy. I want to get out of these jeans."

As soon as they entered his room, Carlos pushed Sebastian towards the bed and yanked his own jeans down. His underwear came down just as quickly, and before Sebastian could adjust himself on the bed, Carlos was on top of him.

"I want to face-fuck you, baby, OK?" Carlos moaned, his sexy accent a little more notable now that he was talking dirty.

Sebastian nodded and slid further under Carlos. He grabbed the gardener's ten-inch shaft with both hands as Carlos braced himself against the headboard. Sebastian led the tip of the big cock to his mouth and Carlos pushed in eagerly.

"Ah, yeah. Hold it in place, buddy," Carlos moaned as he drove his entire dick into the eager mouth. Sebastian started to gag, so Carlos withdrew and leaned down to the young man's face. "Nice. Good boy. Here, kiss me."

To Sebastian, it seemed like they kissed for hours. He loved the way Carlos's rough hands felt on his body, and he really enjoyed being tossed around and told what to do.

Suddenly, Carlos rolled off the bed and was fumbling through his jeans. "Do you have any lube?" he asked, pulling a magnum condom from his front pocket.

"Yeah. Ah … I mean no. Not here," Sebastian said, disappointed.

A smile was plastered on Carlos's face. "That's fine, baby. Here, just turn around. I'll just use my spit. I'll go easy."

Although he was a total bottom, Sebastian was a little apprehensive because his ass was pretty tight—he hadn't had sex for a few months. Still, he turned around and got on all fours, bracing himself for the huge, thick, Hispanic dick that was about to enter him.

He felt Carlos push the tip slowly into his hole and then gently ease the thing in. It seemed to get thicker as it reached the base. Sebastian screamed and buried his face into a pillow.

"Oh, yeah, baby. Come on, take my dick, you little blond bitch," Carlos barked at him. This was Sebastian's first time getting bossed around—well, dominated—and he was really getting into it. Even though he was already struggling to take the entirely of that big dick, the dirty talk sent a surge through his body, causing him to push his ass back against the penetrating cock, sliding it in deeper. After a few seconds, Sebastian felt thick pubes brushing his ass cheeks. Carlos was balls deep. Sebastian screamed out in pleasure and pain.

Carlos was now muttering something in Spanish, which almost pushed Sebastian over the edge. "Oh, Carlos. Yeah! Make me your little bitch. I'll do whatever you want. Ahhhh … *ahhhh …!*" He was moaning, as loud as ever, and Carlos pushed his face back into the pillow. He screamed into it, his ecstasy now uncontrollable, as the larger Hispanic man completely dominated his body with the doggy-style fuck.

"Have you ever been fucked by a man this big, Sebastian? Huh, boy? Have you? Answer me."

"No, sir. Not as big as you. I can barely take it—" he moaned as he lifted his head from the bed. Carlos pushed it back down.

Sebastian glanced to the side and saw their bodies reflected back in the mirror. Carlos's huge and meaty ass was going nonstop, and Sebastian watched as his own body took every one of the man's thrusts, pushing his stomach closer to the unmade bed.

"Do you like my thick cock, man? Let's see how much more I can get in there …" Carlos continued to drive his member into Sebastian, and both were getting closer to a climax. It turned Sebastian on to hear Carlos's manly grunts and moans in his ear. Sure, he was masculine and muscular, too, but one of his fantasies was to be dominated by a larger and stronger man.

It was only his first day back, but Sebastian knew he wasn't going to forget this trip to Los Angles.

"All right, man, let's get you on your back," Carlos said as he withdrew from Sebastian's ass. He flipped him over quickly and plunged his dick back into his waiting hole.

Sebastian's eyes got wide as he looked up at Carlos. Sweat was pouring from his body and his neck was red from the heat. Sebastian slowly lifted his legs and rested them on Carlos's shoulders, then pulled the man in deeper by grabbing his meaty ass and pulling it towards him.

Carlos continued to plow into Sebastian's tight ass, and without warning, he felt the urge to cum. Sebastian instinctively reached for his own cock and began stroking vigorously. He wanted to cum with Carlos.

As he withdrew from Sebastian's hole, Carlos pulled off his condom and tossed it to the side. "Come over here," he said, grabbing the thirty-four-year-old by the neck and jerking his cock at the same time.

Just as Sebastian began to cum, Carlos let out a manly moan and directed the young bottom to open his mouth.

As hot jizz squirted from Sebastian's dick, a thick and heavy stream of it landed on Carlos's beautiful face. Carlos, meanwhile, jerked his own meat, expertly aiming his own load into Sebastian's mouth. After a minute, and some heavy panting, Carlos shoved his semi-hard cock past Sebastian's lips and into his hungry mouth, which immediately went to work sucking the rest of the cum from the still-massive dick.

"Whoooa, baby! Now that's what I call a fuck," Carlos said, laughing to himself. He pulled his dick out and bent down to kiss Sebastian on the forehead.

"Shit, yeah … that was nice," panted Sebastian, cum dripping from the corner of his mouth. "My ass is still feeling it."

"Good," Carlos smirked. "You have a nice tight ass, son. Felt fucking amazing." He pulled on his pants and motioned to the used condom on the floor. "Now don't forget to clean that up," he winked as he opened the door. "I'll grab my check and let myself out."

Sebastian sat there for a moment, dazed, thinking about what had happened. He glanced over at the digital clock on his desk and a small wave of anxiety washed over him. It was 3:17 p.m.

"Shit," he said as he jumped up and made his way back to his bathroom. "Time for another shower."

COLLEGE HUNKS HAUL JUNK
David Aprys

By the ninth take, I'm ready to call the whole thing off.

Who'd have guessed that reality shows are made so painstakingly, and by such fucking perfectionists? Seriously. If Shawn, the tightly-wound director, tells me one more time that I've missed my mark, I'm gonna punch him in the face.

And *I'm* supposed to be the obsessive-compulsive one here.

"Mr. McKenna," says Alyssa, the assistant producer with a kind voice. "Are you ready to try again?"

She stands just out of the shot. Cameras one and two keep rolling.

I eye Dr. Greg Dwyer, who's supposed to be guiding me through this whole process. Fake, of course. Not the doctor—he really is my therapist. But my healing process began six months ago. I've already had my breakthrough.

"Yeah, I'm ready," I answer with a downward glance, looking glum for the cameras. Really I'm side-eyeing one of the movers, who's been scoping me ever since he and his crew arrived at my loft.

His hair is shaggy, somewhere between light brown and red. The auburn beard doesn't hide his square jaw or adorably handsome face. Great smile. His wide shoulders and amazing ass caught my attention the minute he walked in. He's the crew chief of four college-age guys the producers hired to haul away my excess stuff. Think I heard the mover with the buzz cut—the one who's always scowling—call him Kyle.

"Tyler," says the doc, "which one of the bicycles do you want to keep?"

I step forward to the masking tape X mark on the floor. "I ride the blue bike to work. I'd like to keep the red one as backup. The others can go." The key lights catch what I hope is brave decisiveness.

"Cut. Good take," he says, striding over to high-five me. Except for a couple pickup shots, the "before" segment of another episode of *Design from Disaster* is finished.

Two weeks ago, my 2,500 square foot apartment was a mess—full of junk. It's way better now. I'm kind of a hoarder. Not with lots of old boxes, gross unwashed dishes, and fifty-odd cats. I collect curiosities and have a hard time letting them go. With the people in my life, I have the opposite problem.

My college friend Darren, one of the show's producers, thinks my place—a raw loft in a former factory space in Callowhill—has great "bones." It'll look fabulous, he insists, once the show's designers make it over.

Why not see what happens?

After Josh and I broke up and he moved out, I kept myself busy with commercial acting jobs and giving tours in Philly's historic district. I constantly came across weird castoffs and battered antiques. Along the way, I got interested in rehabilitation. When you can't mend your personal life, maybe you want what you *can* fix. So I refinished twelve dressers, repaired twice as many bicycles.

Then I bought an old jukebox and got it working. One thing led to another—soon I had eight decrepit Wurlitzers.

In the meantime, old issues of the *Enquirer* and other magazines piled up. Books and maps overflowed the shelves. My clothes and shoes must've reproduced, there were so many. The dressers filled up, so I bought old wardrobes too. Before I knew it, I was living in a maze. Somehow, I even ended up with seven rusty baby carriages, ten dressmaker's dummies, and a Steinway piano.

Yeah, I'm a little OCD. The key, Dr. Greg points out, is recognizing that.

Right about now, I recognize an obsession with Kyle's forearms. The way the veins stand out in relief as he hauls away one of three ancient sewing machines I bought at a jumble sale. He's well built, has to be a couple inches taller than me, and I'm nearly six foot. It's a warm day for April, and just as I wonder what his upper body looks like under that blue flannel shirt, he takes it off. Beneath is a gray sleeveless tee, clinging to him in all the right places.

The assistant director handles the final shots, mostly of moving guys hauling away more crap I don't need. Except for Shawn, the rest of the crew has left.

I go upstairs to pack a couple more boxes. Below, I still hear the moving guys. They grunt, hoisting furniture that's going in the truck along with the bicycles and baby carriages. They call each other names when one of them loses his hold, slap each other's denim covered asses.

Even up here, the scent of their sweat hangs in the air. It's athletic, intensely masculine, and I go hard inside my jeans. What I wouldn't give to watch Kyle slowly peel off that tank top.

To take my mind off the pornographic fantasy, I scrub the bathroom floor. I don't go downstairs until I hear the door shut.

When I enter the long living space, Shawn is still there with two of the movers—Kyle and the guy with the cropped hair. They're drinking beers and Buzz Cut glowers, gesturing at me when I get to the bottom of the stairs.

He's conventionally hot, though there's something I don't like in those close-set brown eyes. Buzz Cut takes off his T-shirt, revealing a ripped torso. Not a gym body—his is more a combination of good genes and hard work. I count at least a six-pack on that olive-skinned torso. There's a dusting of silky hair between his smooth pecs, and I can't help wondering what he's packing at the other end of the treasure trail that snakes into his low-rise jeans.

My boner isn't going anywhere. I try to rearrange it, hoping the guys won't notice, but Kyle's eyes immediately stray to my crotch. Buzz Cut takes a swig of Pabst Blue Ribbon and gives me a scowl that could kill.

"Mind if Brandon and Kyle hang?" Shawn asks, running fingers through his crow's nest of brown hair. In his other hand, he holds a fancy new digital camera. "Thought I'd grab a couple extra shots—you guys unwinding, having a couple beers."

I shake my head. "I'd rather unwind by myself."

"C'mon, have a beer—chill," says Kyle, handing me a PBR.

I exhale while popping the top. *What the hell,* I think, guzzling the foamy brew.

Shawn films us goofing, kicking around one of twenty-four soccer balls I collected while coaching a kids team last year. Speaking of teams, the designers are coming Monday morning, so there's very little left in the apartment. Plenty of room to play. I guard the windows, Kyle the long kitchen counter. Buzz Cut switches off between us, seeing where he can score a goal.

My long brown Naugahyde couch and beat-up coffee table are all that's left of the living room furniture, along with the television. Everything else has been tossed or put in storage.

After horsing around, we pop open another beer, drink to all that got accomplished these past two days, and to our unplanned soccer game. Exhausted, I drop onto the middle of the couch. Brandon and Kyle plunk down on either side.

They exchange a look before it happens, just as I realize I've been ambushed. With a righteous little smirk, Buzz Cut—Brandon—puts his mitt on my crotch.

I jump like someone poured hot water on me. Brandon's eyes flash, alternating between what his hand is doing, and Kyle, who's rubbing himself through the front of his Levi's.

"Why don't you guys get comfortable?" Shawn suggests. He's still filming, and it's not a secret to anyone with eyes that he's got a hard-on. He strokes himself through the front of his flat front chinos.

Brandon doesn't have to hear the question twice. With his free hand, he unbuttons his jeans and pushes them over the flaring muscles of his hairy thighs. His cock is already poking out of his red striped boxers.

I shove Brandon's hand out of the way and before I can think about it, my pants are around my ankles. Brandon slides his palm over the flat of my belly, reaches inside my underwear, and grabs my dick.

Other than mine, no hand has touched me there in over a year. As more stuff piled up around me, I pushed away chances for human contact. Why did I do that when this feels so fucking good? I squirm, taking in the sensation.

"Yeah, jack him off," Shawn chuckles approvingly.

With a smile on his face, Kyle watches Brandon's fist pumping. He licks his lips, leans closer. In one fluid motion, his mouth joins his friend's hand. They move in tandem on my tool, Brandon stroking the shaft while Kyle tongues the head.

66

I lean back, watching them work. Every cell in my body is waking up, coming back after a long hibernation. I tremble at the feel of Kyle's shaggy reddish hair brushing my thighs. I thrust into Brandon's grip. Then I reach for his dick and start jacking him, too.

"You're wearing way too many clothes," Shawn says, moving his camera closer to the action, still touching himself.

We struggle to get naked. Brandon pulls my Henley over my head after Kyle unbuttons it. I kick off my jeans, my briefs follow them. Then I'm stripping that sweat-soaked Philadelphia Flyers tank top from Kyle's perfect, perfect chest. He's been hauling heavy items all day, but he smells like heaven—clean and fit, virile and evergreen.

Brandon is short, thickset like a wrestler. Kyle, while nearly as muscular, has a rugby player's body—powerful, dangerously sculpted. The brown hair on his chest makes a cross shape, extending in a thick line down his ripped, hard belly. I follow that path with my tongue, taste his salty skin, yank the boxer briefs over his brawny flanks. He steps out of them, stands next to the couch.

I look to Brandon, who's lying on his side. He's naked too, cock jutting straight out from between his ridiculously well-developed thighs. He strokes himself one-handed, using the other to guide my throbbing prick into his mouth.

And me? My mouth is watering for Kyle. He stands over me, a Viking god with shoulders three feet wide. He gives me a generous, sideways grin as I boldly take his cock in my hand. Pre-cum leaks from the pinkish head as it bobs under my touch. Narrowing my eyes, I lick the clear fluid away, wet the shaft with my tongue before taking it into my mouth. He tastes amazing. I watch his face change while sucking him.

I'm on my back, skin sticking to the couch. Brandon's between my legs, giving me head, stroking his big dick. I wouldn't mind having it in my mouth, but I have a higher challenge. Kyle straddles my face, furry thighs on either side of my head. His balls, fragrant with his male scent, dangle towards my mouth.

I jack his cock, sticky with pre-cum and spit. My tongue moistens that sensitive spot just behind his sac. His nuts won't fit in my mouth at the same time, so I take them in turns. He's groaning like a mofo, and I'm afraid he's gonna shoot, so I release his cock. Digging my fingers into his hard thighs, I keep slurping his taint and balls, tease his pucker with my tongue.

"Fuck!" Shawn hollers. "Really hot, guys. Keep it going."

It's a swirl. My dick stretches Buzz Cut's full lips out of shape. Then I hear him licking my balls, picture him stroking himself. Kyle leans forward. His hair and beard brush my bronze thighs as he wedges my meat into his mouth. The feeling is explosive, consuming, and I wonder why I disconnected myself from it for so long.

We reposition ourselves so we're sitting on the couch, legs entwined. I run my hand down Brandon's smooth, ridiculously tight torso and grab his thick cock. I love the sound he makes, grunting like a pig, I'm giving him so much pleasure. He thrusts in my grip, hairy groin slapping my fist. I can tell he's close.

Kyle jacks me slowly, I rest my head against his shoulder. The aroma of his brawny, hirsute body is too much. I train my eyes on his dick while stroking. It dwarfs my hand, pink against the toffee color of my skin.

I'm close now, too; it gathers from all over my body. The muscles of my stomach and ass tense. Kyle feels it as well. Just as I'm ready to explode, he opens his mouth and falls on my cock, still jacking it. At the feel of his coarse beard on my loins, I shoot, plunging my juddering cock into his greedy mouth.

Brandon's head waggles from side to side. His neck strains,

every vein standing out as I stroke him furiously, my arm slick with his sweat. Then he shoots, too. Hot jizz arcs into the air, burns my skin, hits the couch, shoots Brandon in his snub-nosed face. He grimaces with lust.

And I'm still cumming, emptying myself into Kyle's mouth, over his face. Spunk gets in his hair, drips into his beard. Something about that sight makes me shoot another salvo—like a double orgasm.

Shawn kneels just on the other side of the coffee table, cock sticking through the fly of his pants. He jacks himself while filming us. This won't be professional porn—judging by the way his whole body shakes.

Kyle kneels between Brandon and me, tastes the cum on Brandon's skin, licks sweat from my chest. He strokes himself like he's in no hurry.

"Come on, shoot your load, stud," Shawn croons, jockeying for an unobstructed shot.

"Shut the fuck up," Kyle snarks, giving us an unreadable smile.

When he's ready, he stands.

A roar tears from Kyle's throat. He throws back his head with the force, his rocket-shaped cock spewing thick ropes of sperm all over us. He shudders, shakes, straddling our tangled legs. Eagerly, we catch the last threads in our mouths, tongues sparring over the sticky head of his massive cock.

Damn, he tastes as good as he smells. Like cream, fresh grass, and honey. Brandon and I share Kyle's seed with him, kiss him lingeringly. He collapses atop us.

Shawn has edged close to film the big guy's money shot. Now he can't hold back any longer. He fires onto the scarred table top, quaking as the last pearly drops bead on the veneer. Barely making a sound, he zips up in a practiced move moments after shooting.

"Fucking amazing, boys." A smile is on his narrow face, his hair's even more of a crow's nest than before.

Afterwards, Brandon cleans up in the bathroom. Shawn tucks a wad of cash into the pocket of a crumpled pair of jeans while Kyle struggles into his striped boxer briefs, his back to us.

"Guess I'll shower at home." Kyle turns, smiles at me sheepishly. "Oughta splash some water on my face first."

I can't help returning his infectious grin, but doubt takes root as he heads to join his buddy.

"You're not just paying them to haul junk from my apartment, are you?" I ask Shawn once Kyle's out of earshot.

"More like paying them to haul *your* junk," Shawn admits with a raised eyebrow. "Look, Darren arranged for more than the apartment makeover. Said it's high time you got some. And one of these dudes is a pro," he cocks his head towards the bathroom. "This is just his day job."

The pit of my stomach drops. No wonder Kyle looks like that, smells so good, cums like gangbusters. How humiliating. Now I really do want to punch Shawn. Darren, too.

Instead, I make myself scarce. Showering in the upstairs bathroom, I never hear the three of them leave.

I come downstairs to find a scrap of paper on the concrete kitchen counter. Though I barely know Shawn, I assume it's his chicken scrawl, until I see the letter K beneath the words. THAT WAS FUN. KEEP ME IN MIND. There's a phone number too, but I toss the message in the trash before taking note of it.

See, I can throw things away now.

Thursday afternoon five weeks later I see the truck again.

I'm leading a tour group away from Christ Church, the final stop on their excursion through the Old City. Next to Independence Mall, at the corner of Arch and 5th, is a red, white, and blue Econoline box van. On the side is the company's name: COLLEGE HUNKS HAUL JUNK.

Great. That's the company Kyle, the part-time hustler, works for.

I answer a question from the requisite tour douche—a middle-aged history teacher who must've corrected me at least ten times during this, my last walking tour of the day. There's one in every group, I think. But my mind is elsewhere.

Really, there's not much chance Kyle is actually in that truck. After all, the company has vans all over Philadelphia. Last month, when moving in the new furniture, they sent a different crew of guys, thank God. A couple of them were hotties, but no repeat shenanigans for Shawn to film.

Which reminds me. Gotta get my hands on that video. What the hell was I thinking?

I say good-bye to my group, shake hands, get several generous tips. Excellent, because I don't get paid for my latest commercial until next week.

Crossing Arch Street, across from Constitution Center, I notice the moving truck is still there. I approach. Not that I want to get closer, but my bike is chained up on the racks at the north side of Independence Mall.

Lucky me. My bike is about fifty feet from that truck.

A couple of dudes in jeans and company tees are loading broken mall park benches into the College Hunks truck. I remember one of them from the original group of four who took away my excess stuff. Then I see a flash of chestnut hair and beard. Sure enough, coming down the brick walkway with a park official is Kyle.

He hands the parks guy something to sign on a clipboard. When the man passes it back, Kyle spots me and smiles. Shit. Now he's waving.

I stare at my bike lock, pretend I can't figure out the combination.

"Hey Tyler," he says.

I don't look up. My chest tightens, just hearing him speak my name.

"So, you're ignoring me?" he asks, and I now I do look up, lightheaded. "I mean, I get that after what happened you might not have the highest opinion of me. But I still thought maybe you'd call."

"Yeah well, thanks for leaving your number," I dither, tossing a leg over the bike. "Just not sure we have much in common."

His face falls with genuine disappointment. "Can I ask why?"

"Listen, you're a nice guy, Kyle, but I'm not really looking to hang with anyone, let alone a guy who makes his living—"

"Moving stuff? Seriously, because I'm blue collar?" He's gone red in the face, like an angry, adorable little boy. One who is taller than me and has a beard, but still.

"Not that," I lower my voice. "But like, my friend paid you to—"

"*That's* the problem?" he interrupts again, laughing hoarsely. "They hired *Brandon*—Shawn and your friend. I just got all caught up in the sexy. Besides, I couldn't let him have you all to himself. Especially not when—"

"When what?" Now it's my turn to interrupt. I look into those hazel eyes.

"Not when I wanted you all to myself," he says.

Now my face flames, and I smile.

At six-thirty Friday evening, I meet him outside the proud orange walls of Citizens Bank Park. Phillies are playing the Mets. Turns out Kyle's an even bigger fan than I am, and has season tickets.

We get a couple overpriced beers and head to our pavilion seats. But we don't end up watching the game very closely. Mostly we talk and laugh.

Kyle's the same age as me. He started the moving business with his dad four years ago, right after he graduated from Temple University. Staring at his hands, he tells me his dad passed away last winter. Now Kyle's brother works with him. They give college dudes a way to earn honest cash. Brandon grew up in their working-class Kensington neighborhood, moved to L.A. a few years ago, fell in with the wrong crowd. He still does some shady things to make money now that he's clean and back home.

We devour roast pork sandwiches and have another beer. I tell him my dad took off when I was a kid. How hard my mom worked to give me a good life. How much I miss her now that she's gone.

Even in the crowded ballpark, Kyle's not self-conscious. His strong hand brushes against mine. After the seventh inning stretch we decide to leave. The Phillies are losing anyway.

We have to change trains twice to get to Callowhill. It's almost ten o'clock when we walk in the door of my new digs. Well, I've lived here five years, but now it's new.

Kyle whistles with appreciation. "Different," he says, "but way nice."

I step aside, let him look around. Shining refinished wood floors, whitewashed pillars. Roman blinds hang at the long windows. Warhol, de Kooning, and Ellis Wilson reproductions have replaced tacky posters. My two bikes are housed on proper racks under the staircase. Only one jukebox survived the transition.

It's cool for mid-May, and he wears a thick wool hoody. "Can I take your sweater?" I ask, my voice hollow in this minimalistic space, my stomach full of butterflies.

Kyle takes off the hoody and hands it over, his chest as broad as summer is long. He smells fresh, of Zest and clean hair.

When I peer into the closet, my mouth goes dry. Apparently,

I've gotten rid of all the spare hangers, so I toss his sweater across the arm of the couch. The one where the two of us and Brandon …

Awkward.

He raises an eyebrow, smirks. Those aren't butterflies in my stomach. More like giant moths.

Kyle trails me into the kitchen. I open up two Yuenglings. He stands so close I can feel the heat from his body. He takes the beer, stretches his broad shoulders, and hides a yawn.

"Got any coffee?" he asks.

"I'm more a tea drinker." I hesitate. "There might be some instant Folgers?"

He masks a laugh with the back of his hand. "Whatever you've got."

These moths are getting restless. I don't trust myself to speak, so I start the kettle and search the cabinet, finding the coffee behind a clear plastic bag full of sugar.

"Milk?" I ask, stirring in two heaping spoonfuls of sweet stuff. He nods and I add that, too. We make for the couch.

I can tell something's wrong when he takes the first sip. His face folds in on itself. Before I say anything, Kyle spews a mouthful of hot coffee all over the couch, all over both of us.

"Salt!" he gasps.

I run to the kitchen for a glass of water. When I return, he's in the bathroom, rinsing his mouth under the shiny modern tap. Afterwards, he wipes his face with a hand towel while I wait for him in the doorway, my stomach roiling.

"You OK?" I ask.

He grunts, frowning into the mirror. Despite my nerves, I want to laugh. But I think better of it as Kyle turns, approaches the bathroom doorway. His intense stare penetrates, like he's got unpleasant news.

74

I step aside so he can exit, but Kyle moves left when I go right. I shimmy left, he dodges right and bumps into me. An uncomfortable dance—one that says this night is a disaster. Stupid me. At the game, I thought *maybe, just maybe.*

"What're you doing?" he asks when I step back.

"Just, you know, getting out of your way." My voice sounds puny.

"I'm trying to kiss you, numbnuts." He gives me that sideways smile.

I freeze for a second. Then he pounces like a tiger and we're grappling in that too narrow doorway. My hands twine behind his neck. He grapples my waist forcefully, seeing if I'll break.

He mauls me with his mouth and hands. I cannot get enough of the way he tastes. We slam into the wall, rip the shirts from each other's bodies. I dig my fingers into firm biceps, run my hands over the swell of his chest. Rusty brown hair scratches my palms. My tongue follows the sinews of his throat to his pecs and finds one rosy nipple. I bite gently, and he pushes it into my mouth. I bite down.

Kyle moans, grinds his hardness against my belly. I'm hard too—unbearably so. He rubs the outline of my dick through my jeans. Then we're in a frenzy, unbuttoning flies, yanking denim over muscled flanks.

Even through ribbed cotton briefs, Kyle's cock is huge. My mouth waters, remembering. I fall to my knees, peeling away his boxer briefs. It points at me, a ruddy, thick, veined creature. I take it between my lips, feel his pulse jumping.

Kyle steadies himself against the wall. I open my throat, let his length slide in. My lips are at the base of his manhood, his coppery bush tickles my nose. I move my head clockwise, rolling his tool in my mouth. His hands grip my head, force his prick down my gorge. Staring up at him, I can't breathe. I'm dizzy, in awe. He pulls out slowly, rams himself back in, repeats until the tears stream down my face and sweat slicks his torso.

We trade. I stand while he kneels, licks my cock, strokes it teasingly. Finally he takes it all the way into his mouth. His hands are tight on my butt, guiding. After a couple thrusts, I can't stop. I'm fucking his face.

I look down at him, a brawny bearded stud, eyes trained on mine, stroking himself while he sucks me. A noise that sounds like pain comes from deep inside my throat.

Neither of us are going to last very long. Not at this rate.

Kyle must be thinking the same thing. He lets go of my dick and stands, kisses me again, long and deep. The taste of my loins is in his mouth. Then he pulls back, smiling wickedly. He spins me around and slaps my rump.

"Get upstairs," he growls. "This time, I'm gonna split that sweet ass in two."

Stark naked, I run for the stairs. Kyle shadows me, close on my heels.

The minute my feet hit the shaggy bedroom area rug he's on me. He grabs my shoulders, shoves me face forward onto the bed. In a trice, Kyle positions himself behind me. His hands take my hips, coax me onto all fours. He slaps my ass again—harder—and spits into my crack. He spreads me apart, gets me wet with his fingers. With his other hand, he brushes rough knuckles against the underside of my dick.

Kyle doesn't waste time. He slides in the tip, reaches around, pinches both my nipples. I think I'm going to burst. He rumbles in his throat, pushes farther. I cry out with the revelation. *How did I wait so long to let myself be vulnerable again?*

He guides us both, thrusting in and out, restraining my movements. With each rush forward his breathing changes. I cede to his authority, know he's losing control, that for now we're both in a world he built. Before long, animal noises escape us, and he's deeper inside me than anyone ever has been.

I need to see his face, have to know whether this thing controlling us is real, or just for an hour. The second I'm on my back, I know. It's not something I see, though it shows in his expression. It's in the air between us. When Kyle lunges forward, sinks into our shared hunger, I meet him, anticipating his every move.

I fight back ecstasy as he drives me with ruthless force. His golden mane sticks to his face and neck, our sweat mingles. He slams me brutally, I beg for more, push back against him. Inside me is a growing heat. I knot my ankles at the small of Kyle's back, taking all of him.

We kiss, mouths engulfing each other. His hand pistons my aching cock. I'm ready to shoot—can tell he is, too. *Don'tpulloutdon'tpullout,* I think, mind scrambling. He doesn't.

Then he's cumming, and I feel it. He throbs inside me, hitting a place I'd forgotten—where I live. Kyle's face contracts with torment, with pleasure. His body convulses, his lungs wrench out a massive groan.

I explode in Kyle's hand, sending geysers of cum all over us. Shuddering, I can't stop. I'm losing consciousness—wave after wave of golden fire consumes me. Each muscle in my body connects with his cock, and I watch his face change. He smiles, grimaces, loses himself utterly.

He collapses, whispering dirty words I don't really hear. My mind flutters near the impossibly high ceilings of this room. I squeeze Kyle with all my strength. We roll into an unbroken kiss as the afterglow fades and we're left with heavy limbs.

He's surprised when I ask him to stay. But like Dr. Greg says, the only way to overcome fear is to open myself to new possibilities.

And this is a new possibility.

I crawl into Kyle's arms, thrill to the sound of his breathing getting deeper. My hand crawls across the expanse of his chest.

"We gotta get you a decent coffee maker tomorrow," he mumbles, just before I drift off to sleep. Long pause.

"And some sugar."

MORE THAN MEETS THE EYE

Landon Dixon

It was a scene right out of one of those detective digests. Or was it?

Good-looking doll poured into a neon-red dress and snow-white silk stockings strolls into my office and husks, "I've got a job for you, Mr. Dawson. I want you to fuck my wife, and take pictures, too."

Instantly, there was something wrong with this picture, whet as it was, and this whole scene. Did "she" say "wife"? In 1959 Toronto?

My parched tongue clogged my dry gulch throat. I blinked orbs more red-veined than a rummy's nose. I'd gone twenty-four hours without sleep and whiskey, working a case. And now this?

I grated, "Your wife?"

The doll had one of those oval faces perfect for framing cameo-style, velvet brown eyes that flickered with fire, and satin black hair that flaunted in waves, a button nose and pincushion lips. Her pretty face was adorned with vibrant blue eye shadow and glossy red lipstick, lashes extended and curled like the heated, bent tines of a comb.

She sauntered around my desk right up to me sprawled out in my chair like a bus depot bum. The vapor trail of her sweet, warm perfume washed over me in waves a split second later. I ogled her sensuous kisser, her curvy physique, her shapely stems, the depths of her cleavage and the heights of her breasts.

She was some siren, all right, stutted up on five-inch shiny red stilettos. She went off, "That's right ... Tom. My wife."

She untucked a snapshot from her black leather clutch and disced it down into my lap. I caught it up, gandered the photo. My interest was plenty aroused between both my legs and ears now. "Herzzoner!" I gulped.

The picture portrayed the first female mayor of Hogtown. At her swearing-in ceremony circa May 15, '59. Two weeks whence.

But before I could launch another choked query, the doll slid the floss straps of her red-alarm frock off her burnished bronze shoulders. Revealing an equally packed-with-potential red satin bra. "That's right, Tom," she whispered again. "Her Worship Chris Clair and I were married in the First Galactic Church of Canada. It's as real as any other marriage, to those who believe in the Celestial Sensations. To remain unbroken between humanoids except in certain extreme cases—like adultery."

When did the TTC crazy train add a stop at my door, I wondered?

I let that question lie when the doll's dress flipped down to her waist along with my mind. Her skin was smooth and tan all over, her bellybutton cute as a lovebug's ear. She unlatched the loaded bra at the back and let fly.

My eyes widened clear to Sarnia and my dick crawled up my groin in earnest. Her tits were firm, round balls of fun-time, topped by joyously jutting nipples. "Got a name, toots?" I managed to grunt.

"I call them 'the twins,'" she giggled. Then soothed, "Sam Torrance." She slipped down to her sweet little knees.

She'd got the drop on me, and I spread 'em wide—my legs. She unhooked my belt and unbuttoned my fly without so much as snagging a red-lacquered nail, obviously some experience with guys as well as gash. She gasped when she peeped the black lace panties I was sporting that day.

"Soooo …" she murmured, grasping my rigored dick in its sexy lace casing and stroking with her soft, slender, warm hand.

"That's cocking the hammer," I muttered, surging hard as the cobblestones out on Yonge Street.

The scanties were courtesy of Lasha, my loyal secretary. The fetish was yours truly. Sam's technique was pure pleasure, the doll jacking my chamber with a practiced precision, fondling my shaven balls with her other hand. The sensation of sheer lace and hot skin was something I live for.

But I live also to pay the bills. So I mouthed, "Make love to the mayor, huh? That could get hairy. What's your angle?"

The words tripped over my tongue and gushed out of my mouth with a full pint of drool as Sam slipped Lasha's panties aside and pumped my cock and balls bare and barehanded. She tossed back her long, night-shaded tresses, bowed her perfectly made-up face down, and gave my nuts a firm lick, looking up at me with glittering glims.

"Chris is planning to divorce me. I want to strike first, raise a big stink. She wants to dump me now that she's a big politico … and I'm a liability. So I want you to pound out the evidence of adultery I'll need to settle her score."

She put her twisted tongue back to better use, swirling it all around my balls. While she hand-pumped my stiffness with just the right pressure and wrist-snap. This doll was damn handy with a man's pork and beans, despite her avowed all-fish diet.

"Blackmail, huh?" I groaned, my balls tightening and cock surging, nipples twinkling like pink stars in Lasha's brassiere. I reached down to the sides and gripped the doll's tits, groped. Her chest-balls were firm, plenty firm for a dame pushing forty.

Sam bent my rod down and poured her pouty red lips over my dinking cap, glided her hot, damp mouth down half of my barrel. I let go of her tits and flopped back in my chair.

Her eyes shone on high-beam in front of my own spinning sighters as she squeezed my wettened balls with her hand and wet-vacced my cock with her mouth, bobbing her head back and forth, sucking like she was starving for foreskin. Her oral technique was flawless as well, damn highly flammable. She knew just where the hot spots were located on a man's molten length—everywhere, of course, but especially just below the hood, where her tongue gave an extra sweet swirl with each lip-dragging pull. I burned inside and out, hitting Fahrenheit Fucking Incredible.

I had to pull the doll up onto my lap before I spontaneously combusted liquid lust down her throat. She suddenly squirmed, struggling, surprising me all over again.

But my hands held firm and my hard-on firmer. I shoved her dress up and shunted her red satin panties aside, not about to be deprived when so provoked. And that's when I got shocked right down to the rocks. Because this "doll" came equipped with a big, hard cock, bobbing right down there between her shaven loins for me to peep. Sam was a she-male, a transsexual, halfway there to the change-up Christine Jorgensen had so brashly initiated seven years earlier.

"Hot rod!" I breathed, gaping at the throbbing stretch of man-dom, the heaving jugs and curvaceous bod and blushing face of a feminine.

My own cock surged with this new, unexpected development—like its sometimes master, never one to back down from a challenge.

I gripped the fag-pole and started stroking. Sam tilted her head back and moaned, her tresses cascading, her tits jumping. Her prick pulsed mightily in my shunting hand, thick and heavy and heated, all-man every inch. I had to taste it to be sure, though, and I did. Like any good, sleazy private dick, I never leave any cock or cajones unturned.

I hiked Sam higher up in my chair, so that her slut heels were standing up on my armrests, her hard-on stuck out right in front of my face. I gripped her narrow waist. She grabbed onto my natty hair. I said "Ah" and she said "Oh!" as I slid my thick lips over her thick cap and started sucking.

"Oh, God! Yes, Tom!" she gulped in a voice with more than a trace of the masculine.

I pulled tight and wet on her cap, looking up along the curvy length of her femme body, down along the corded length of her homme hammer. Her cock head was just the right amount of chewy as I bit into it. She arched up above me. I shot my hands onto her shuddering tits and grabbed hold, sliding my mouth down almost the entire stretch of her shaft.

Her cock was as rock-hard real as it gets, beating in my heated mouth, between my sealing lips. This lady-boy came equipped with the torrid tools to bend any straight man to her/his passion— and for a guy as crooked me, it was a thrill-and-a-half to mouth prick and handle tits all in one helping. I bobbed my head back and forth, blowing Sam's pipe like she'd wet-vacced my hose.

She shivered and squealed and pumped her hips, feeding me more of the good stuff. I sucked air through my nostrils and cock through my mouth, diving down as much dong as I could and then pulling back with pneumatic intensity. Her cock filled my face, shunting in and out of my cake-hole in rhythm.

Then I abruptly pulled back, disgorging her dick. She quivered above me, her dong twitching in front of me. Time for a nut job. I jumped out my tongue and jabbed it in between Sam's legs, jounced her balls with the tip. She jerked and squawked, cock vibrating like a sexual tuning fork.

I swabbed her sac with my licker, feeling it tighten under my eager, moist swipes. There was semen in there thar balls, I could feel it—and see it, leaking out the mushroomed tip of Sam's boiled length. I gobbled up her sac in one hearty gulp and sucked, pulling on her boy-bag with my lips, swirling my tongue all around the stubbled lumps.

Until Sam suddenly humped back, uncorking her dripping balls from my mouth with a wet pop. She glared down into my upturned eyes. "Fuck me!" she hissed.

I grinned, brought the dish back down to lap level. Then I yanked a desk drawer open and grabbed up a tube of lube and gallantly greased my raging erection. I took a couple of slippery swipes in between Sam's truly taut butt cheeks, too, just to be chivalrous and sure.

She shuddered, delighted. I busted my cap into her hole and blasted tube steak right up her cute little ass. Her own shiny cock shook like a hog's leg when you rub its belly.

"Now I'll take the case," I gritted, gripping the doll's tits and pumping up into her anus. "Since we're not hiding any secrets."

She bleated with glee, grasping my rugged shoulders and bouncing up and down in my lap, on my dong, her own cock bounding right along to the frenzied beat.

The chair creaked and our sex-heated flesh slapped together. We breathed fast and hard, like my cock churning and burning Sam's chute. I squeezed her heavy tits and spun her rubbery nipples, quickly pistoning past the point of no sperm return. Sam's anus was just too tight and too hot, the stunning contrast of striking cockiness and sterling femininity too much for me.

84

"Fire in the hole!" I hollered.

Sam popped her eyes open and unlatched a set of nails from my shoulder, gripped and ripped her own jerking cock, riding high and hard on my pommel. I spasmed and shot, blowing my balls out with orgasm. And I swear Sam's pert, depthless rump sucked on my rupturing pipe as I sprayed, as she jacked steaming jizz out of her own erupting hose and all over the both of us.

We hardly had time to catch our breath in each other's mouths, our tongues twining together like serpents again—when Lasha burst into my private office and blasted away with a Colt 45. The pony gun bucked up and down in her thrust-out hands, spraying hot lead all over the place. All the while screaming, "You bastard! You fuck all your clients, but you won't fuck me!"

Hell hath no fury like a woman not porned.

But while her sentiments were on-target, thank Jehovah, her aim was not. Her bullets of rebuffed rage buzzed harmlessly past us and burrowed in the walls and my calendar of pin-ups.

All except one flesh-seeking missile, which struck Sam in the neck. The doll was flung tighter into my arms by the impact. The chair and the pair of us went over like sunken ships in the night.

"She's unconscious, weak, but she'll live," Lieutenant Jackson drawled in his monotone, barring me from the hospital room where Sam slept.

He shoved his fedora back with a nicotine-stained thumb and gave me the wary once-over and under, with his ice-blue eyes. A hard man, with a hard, bony face and hard, bony body, Roman nose and Stone Age chin and attitude. Immaculately attired, as usual, in a dark blue power suit and pink silk tie, white shirt bright enough to give you the third degree, black leather shoes polished to mirrors on the hoof.

"Why'd Lasha blast her? What's the doll's story—your case?" He grimaced. "Lasha ain't talking. She's loyal to you, God knows why. I'm gonna hold you as a material witness unless you spill with some answers, Dawson."

I figured that, figured more. "Is there somewhere we can jaw—man-to-man? Put our heads together on this thing?"

Jackson's emotionless eyes flickered, and some color warmed his normally cold, pallid face. He hesitated, then jerked his thumb at a supply closet across the hall.

We both had broken our dicks out before the door closed and the lights flickered on. Then we really did put our heads together—our cock heads—me gripping our manly appendages and pumping the pair together to full and flagrant inflation.

Jackson groaned, grabbed onto my shoulders, his eyelashes flouting the air like we were flouting the law. He swarmed his heavy, wet tongue into my open, waiting mouth. We thrashed our talk-tools together, as I rubbed our fuck-sticks as one throbbing long mass.

I knew the cock-skimming session would only buy me a day or two. But a day or two was all I needed to get to the bottom and booty of this case. See, I work fast.

Jackson sunk his sharp teeth into my tongue and sucked with his thin lips. Quick and tight as I was jacking our dongs. He quivered, his strong, hot hands shaking my shoulders. For all his dispassionate demeanor, the guy had a horny hair trigger.

"Jesus, Tom! I'm cumming!" he cried in my mouth.

We shook as a team, joined at the dicks, my hand a blur on our o'erheated hard-ons. Then Jackson bucked wild, and I felt his sizzling sperm splash my groin. That was my trigger. I shot the works against his jumping groin, along the guy's joyously spasming shaft.

And then I started to believe Sam's story—when I exited the

supply closet with a smile and saw Herzzoner slipping into the doll's hospital room for a semi-surreptitious visit.

I was a big-money backer with more pork than I knew how to barrel. Chris Clair and I shook hands in her brand new office down at city hall. While Shorty, my shutterbug, captured the moment on film for posterity.

Then I pretended to shoo Shorty out of the office for a closed-door session with Herzzoner. Only, when the mayor turned her back to walk to her desk, and while I shielded little Shorty with my big body, the pint-sized photog slid in behind a potted plant next to the door and took up position for ambush.

"Well, Mr. Dawson, you said you wanted to discuss a real estate redevelopment proposal?"

Chris Clair was a cute little thing. Around forty years old, with a tight, trim figure, bobbed, blonde hair and a pale, squarish face set with sparkling, green eyes and capped with a firm, dimpled chin. She looked downright delectably demanding in the open-for-civic-business dressing she had on—a short, black, wool frock that was neither too loose nor too tight, fully capable of molding to her bouncy body and hemmed high enough to fully show off her black stockinged gams, the two-inch black pumps strapped to her small peds. A pair of silver hoop earrings and a string of white pearls set off the lady-in-charge ensemble to good effect. It was having a good effect on me, deep down in the pit of my groin.

I shut the door and strode over to her desk.

"That's right. I'm willing to spend millions on a new housing development in the Kensington area. Raze the old and raise the new. Increase property values and taxes big time." I grinned pearly whites of my own, shined specially for the occasion. "And I'm willing to spend some more ... to ensure I get the rezoning I need."

Chris's eyes twinkled like dollar signs. Her fingers laced together on top of the desk to keep her palms from itching too much.

My grin spread like oil on water. Politicians are all the same, no matter what their political stripe, or gender-bent. "Why don't I lay my cards on the table?"

"Please do."

I unwrapped my cock from my pants and shorts and stretched the trenching tool across Her Worship's desk. Eight solidifying inches of pure pork.

Chris's orbs danced from my laid-out length to that equally tempting laid-out offer of mine. "How much more are you willing to spend?" she breathed.

"Twenty mil on the housing project, a hundred thousand for the politico who can shepherd the project through all of the hoops in the three-ring circus you got going on down here." I looked down at my last offer. "Cock free of charge—to seal the deal."

Chris licked her lips. Then she stood up and strutted decisively around the desk, curved her hand down over my snake. "We have a deal."

I kissed the mayor, hard. She was as wet and dewy as new-minted money. She clutched up my pipe and pumped it with her warm little hand. I pushed her wool dress down over her buff shoulders and struck bra. I gathered up her heated treasure chest as our lips played together, her hand tugging out a tune of pure delight on my pulsating skin flute.

Her white cotton cup holders fell down to the carpet, revealing white little mounds tipped by taut little pink nipples. I cupped them, fondled the fun-loving pair, flicked her nipples to full-out rigidity. Chris moaned into my mouth, her hand swirling up and down my cock, burnishing me to steel-like hardness.

I broke away from her pink mouth and dove my gourd down

to her pink buds. I sucked most of one tit into my mouth, vacced like a Hoover, did the same with heady relish to her other lovely chest-hump. She shivered, pulling as urgently on my prong as I was mouthing her mams.

"I want to fuck you!" I rasped.

"Yes, fuck me!" she pleaded her agreement, willing to compromise anything. Like any good politician worth their weight in glib.

I spun her around and pushed her up against a chair, sideways for Shorty. Then I shoved up the clinging hem of her dress, skimming taut, creamy buttocks. She shouted, "Fuck my ass! I don't want to get pregnant!"

Always thinking of her duty to her constituents. It was a reasonable request, which would do the job just as well.

I oiled my cock with the grease I carry around in a vial as Chris wrenched her white cotton panties to one side, fully exposing her perky back mounds. Then she reached back with both hands and spread the two cheeky flaps, bending over the chair, exposing her pink pucker.

I gripped my lubed lance and charged forward like the Heavy Brigade, spearing starfish and blossoming same. I downed half my jack-handle into her chute, making the both of us shudder and moan.

Then I held the hardcore position, half-buried in Herzzoner's butt. I grunted, "Shoot, yes!"

That was Shorty's cue. He jumped out from behind the potted plant like a lecherous leprechaun. He held his hard little cock in one hand, his mini-camera in the other. The sawed-off, paid-off pervert shot with both one-eyes, snapping some pics and spurting much jizz.

I kept Chris occupied with her eyes shut and body shaking, slowly and sensuously sinking the rest of my spelunker into her anus. The fit was air and breath-tight, hot as damnation. I gripped her hips and poured fuel onto our raging fires, donging back and forth in her chute.

Shorty zipped and stowed and gave me the high-sign. Then he slipped out of the office like a dirty shadow, unnoticed by the mayor, soon to be cursed by the carpet-cleaner.

Chris had her hands and ass full, holding tight to the rocking chair, getting banged like a gong with all of my thundering cock up her butt. I drove her like the par five at Scarboro—hard and long and straight down the middle, with plenty of body english and good ball bounce.

She tore a hand off the chair and dove it down to her groin. She spasmed, arching up on the end of my ass-chugging cock, crying out her cumming.

And then things got even hairier when she jumped her steaming rump off my tunneling prick and I gandered the strips of sperm "Chris" had laid down across the seat of the chair while I'd been searing her seat. Herzzoner wasn't a her—she was half a he, like her "husband," my client, Sam. She spun around and I hung a shocked look on her hung cock.

"Now, how about some payback?" she said with a smile. "To really seal our deal?"

Her dong jutted straight out from her clean-shaven groin, a pearl of cum glazing the gaping slit. It was my turn to bend over backwards, to play foul ball. I tossed Chris the lube and took up position, gripping the arm of the chair, bobbing my big butt up in back.

Apparently, she was not only a political up-and-comer, but also a sexual multiple-cummer. She hit me hard with the head of her cock. I pushed back. Her cap bust my ass ring and shot inside of my chute, followed by every sinking inch of her swollen shaft.

I grunted, my knuckles burning white on the chair, my ass

blazing full of cock. Chris dug her fingernails into my waist and pumped her hips, bouncing her thin thighs off my full cheeks, pistoning my stretched anus with her plunging dong. She was used to back-door dealings, it was obvious, good at it. I grabbed onto my own flapping steel and stoked.

I jacked happily and hurriedly, pulling hard on my prick. As Chris slammed into my ass at ramming speed. Then she shrieked and bucked on the end of my butt. I felt white lightning strike my bowels repeatedly. I arched my ass and back and bellowed my own ecstasy out of my mouth and blasted it out of my cock, striping that mayoral chair with a second coat of political and testicular goodwill.

I was owed an explanation and a fee. Went hunting for both.

Sam was conscious, although still kind of cobwebby. I woke her fully up when I showed her the skin pics Shorty had shot, told her of the sperm her "wife" had spilled in my ass. The gorgeous creature sighed and came clean.

"Yes, Chris is … like me—a transsexual. No one knows it but me and her aide of long-standing, Steve Gordon. He's actually the one blackmailing her."

She licked her paled lips, her brown eyes showing some life now. "I want you to plant those pictures in Steve's desk at city hall and then phone in an anonymous tip to the police as to where they can find them. They'll arrest Steve for attempted extortion, and the pictures will prove Chris is all-woman to the public—if they're ever made aware of them."

I gave my numbed noggin a shake like you would an overripe coconut. With the same sloshing-sound results. "Huh?"

Sam gripped my hand, put the soft, sexy squeeze on me. "Please, just do it. Chris doesn't know I hired you, but I figured this was the only way to stop Steve from exploiting and spoiling Chris's success. I don't hold it against Chris for fucking with you—that's just part of her job now. I counted on that."

I gaped like a split melon.

"Please, you have to do it! For the good of me and Chris. And Toronto—the good!"

"OK, I'll do it," I said, my civic pride on the line. "So long as you drop all charges against Lasha." She was a jealous girl, my secretary, but one hell of a typist and bill collector, with one wonderful wardrobe. I had a soft spot for her a mile wide, just not a hard spot eight inches long. I was wearing her pink silken bra and panties package as we spoke, as well as two of the dame's ruffled pink garters.

Sam washed my hand with hers. "Done. Chris is good friends with the chief of police." She smiled. "Thanks."

I chased away that pretty grin by dinging the lady-boy with my bill.

Did it all make sense? Who killed the chauffeur in *The Big Sleep?* Who knows? Who cares? Like Marlowe and Hammer before me, mine is not to ask my client why, mine is but to dick and get a piece of the cream pie. Or petoot, in this case.

DUDE FRIDAY

T. Hitman

One of life's great truths, Kevin discovered early that summer, was that a dude boned stiff out of his skull, laid up on the couch with a busted leg, could always jerk his dick as a way to suffer through the boredom and pass the time. And so he did. As the reality set in—a compound fracture to the tibia as a result of a nasty collision on the basketball court right as he readied to take a shot—June and all the fun he'd planned to enjoy over the summer waned. He was stuck. There'd be no wild parties, no long road trips with buddies who had already departed for distant other parts of the country. So far, none of the hot sex he'd counted on had happened apart from a lot of affection from his stroke hand. His only companion was his dick. They were stuck with one another. Kevin had to make the best of the sitch, and tried.

The itch that loved to play hide and seek flared again, this time across the back of his nuts.

"Fuck," Kevin grumbled, still not awake enough to form the word clearly.

He reached down, fingers fumbling through the folds of his cotton shorts. He found his nuts and then zeroed in on the itch. After a few scratches that stirred the sweaty stink of his junk and woke him fully, the itch vanished, only to reappear a few seconds later, this time in that place just out of reach under the hard shell of his cast.

Kevin knew that it was best to ignore the itch, which sometimes took on the appearance of an elf in his imagination, a little fucker with pointy ears that delighted in adding to his misery. It wasn't bad enough that he was laid up in the living room at his dad's apartment with a busted leg that would soon, after healing, make him feel a hundred or older instead of twenty.

The elf dug in its tiny fingers, and the itch migrated. Kevin swore again and reached over to the coffee table for the long flathead screwdriver, which he'd appropriated from one of his father's toolboxes during a bold trip through the place on his crutches. He worked the tip into the top of his cast, which ran from above his left knee down to his toes. The rigid shape made spearing the little fucker through its pointy ear nearly impossible, but he got close, so close. The itch fled; now he was reminded only of the pain, which pulsed from deep within his shattered bones.

He hadn't felt the break in the way that was expected. Dribbling the ball, a pass over from Parmenter, and that nut-tickling rush as he readied to shoot for the basket, all on an afternoon that felt ridiculously effortless and, now, part of some other life. Then the blur had appeared at his periphery, another body perhaps also caught up in the stupid fun of one more game of hoops before summer break. Pedro Saviano then slammed into him, size thirteen sneakers crunching on hairy shin instead of gymnasium floor. Yeah, the crack had shuddered up through the rest of his bones on a wave of pins and needles, enough to leave him flat on his spine, but—

"Shouldn't it hurt more?" Kevin remembered asking. "I don't feel it as much as I thought."

"You will," the ambulance tech had answered, flashing an ominous smirk. "Just wait."

As they'd loaded him in for a ride to the hospital and his double date with the x-ray machine and orthopedic specialist, the pain caught up.

The cast squeezed down again, bottling the heat, conjuring sweat, a prison cell confined to one part of his body but forcing the rest of him to lug it around. The image of the elf had appeared in his mind's eye after taking an extra dose of pain meds. Kevin reached for the bottle on the coffee table that was angled toward him for convenience and knocked down his first dose of the day with a swig of room-temp water. He withdrew the screwdriver and prayed the elf was done fucking with him for the time. It wasn't. An itch ignited between his toes. He did the best he could by flexing them and scratching them over the armrest. Then it was back on his balls. At least Kevin had a level of control there. He scratched. His cock thickened in response, stretching out along the base of his wrist, eager again for attention.

He gave his nuts another tug. Meaty and loose, they threatened to roll down his legs, past the top of the cast, halfway to his ankles. Kevin thumbed at his thatch of pubic hair, caught more of his ripening male scent, and obeyed his dick. After a few stiff strokes, he was dripping.

Another side effect born of his growing boredom, Kevin crooked his neck and chest down, and again attempted to suck his own dick. Gravity dragged on the cast, denying him the privilege. Close—he was so fucking close, he could almost lick the head! Defeated, he slumped back. The rest of the world had moved on and was enjoying the best summer in human history. Only his cock had stayed behind, offering him a distraction.

Kevin licked his finger, tasted the salty nectar leaking from his piss slit, and lubed up his dick's head. Being given a permission slip to lounge on the couch with the remote control wasn't the slice of paradise so many dudes would believe. But jerking off, for however short or long he managed to hold out before nutting, now that was another matter. Among the best. If only he could somehow prolong the electric surge of energy broadcast out of his cock from a handful of seconds into minutes, hours, days.

Kevin unconsciously smiled and thought about his orthopedic specialist, Doctor Olber. The man's handsome face materialized in the space beyond his slitted eyes. Olber was tall, an inch or two past the six-foot mark, an athlete. The way his big hands had run the plaster rolls around Kevin's injured leg was as sensual as it was skilled. At the time, fresh off the campus basketball court, Kevin had been sweaty, so sweaty. The injury did its best to shrink his balls, which the game with his buddies had pumped full of seed. He forgot the pain, remembered how he'd gotten hard with Olber working between his legs, so close to his sac. The warmth of his fingers—if only he'd reached up, shown Kevin's middle leg the same attention he showered on the left.

Kevin pumped his dick. Pre-cum flowed, making the need for spit no longer necessary. In his jerk-off fantasy, what he assumed would only be the first in a long line of bastings to help pass the day, Olber smiled at him. Handsome fucker, with his neat, thinning hair and five o'clock scruff showing early on that fateful afternoon. Dream-Olber reached higher and yanked his briefs aside. Kevin's nuts spilled out, loose and reeking of sweat. He remembered the doctor's voice, a manly baritone. Olber grunted a string of lusty expletives and exhaled a hot breath that rippled over Kevin's balls and the hairs wreathing the root of his shaft.

"Suck it," Kevin moaned. "Suck my fucking cock, Doc!"

Olber's handsome mug moved higher, the older man's mouth aimed at his dick. Closer, closer yet—

The wait of the seconds grew maddening. He thought of how, with each follow up visit to Olber's office, the temptation to go commando beneath his shorts possessed him. To just let his nuts free ball in front of the doctor's face. Maybe then his fantasies would play out in real time as a result.

Energy raced out of his dick's head, up his torso, and down his legs. The first shot of skeet blasted out of his cock and through his fingers. The second splashed Kevin's goatee. A drop of his batter flew into his mouth. He imagined it was Doctor Olber's. The next left a mess across the line of fur that cut down the center of Kevin's chest.

He settled back on the sofa, aware of his curling toes and cooling sperm. Not exactly the way he imagined spending his summer, Kevin sighed yet again. But at least, he had his dick to keep him company.

The worst part about recovering at his dad's apartment was not being able to escape when the arguments started, which were inevitable.

The latest involved his recent lack of hygiene—he was marinating on the couch with a fractured leg and cast, Kevin reminded the old man. Not his fault or how he'd planned to spend his summer. Getting to the bathroom door on crutches was piss-miserable enough, but getting in and out of the tub required an extra set of hands.

"Are you offering to play nurse?" Kevin fired back.

His father grunted something under his breath and slammed his bedroom door, another of those gifts the situation denied Kevin. While he reclined on his spine, aware of the itch's return but too hacked off to acknowledge it, he heard the prick talking on his phone, barking out words, punctuating statements with laughter.

Those phony outbursts fueled his anger. He hadn't asked to be in this predicament and was doing the best he could under the circumstances. There were a million comebacks he wanted to lob at the old man, who didn't need crutches to navigate from one room to another and was free to go from this place any time he chose, to any destination he wanted. But they all jumbled together when his dad returned, and the evil elf seized that moment to tap dance over his left knee. The itch flared. Kevin's father fixed him with a look.

"I hired someone."

"Yeah?" Kevin said and winced. A great comeback flashed through his mind's eye, about the old man finally getting help for his anger management. Another followed—a prostitute to remove the stick from his ass. But they vanished in a maddening rush of discomfort.

"Someone to help you get back and forth, out of the house if you want some air. Take you to your doctor visits. Someone who's gonna wash the stink off you, too."

"I don't need—" Kevin started, only to recant while in mid-sentence. "Fine."

"I think the word you're looking for is 'thanks.'"

"Sure, thanks," he said, knowing it was his only option to surrender.

His father snorted through his nose, evoking an image of an angry cartoon bull. The only things missing were the wisps of smoke drifting out of his nostrils. The battle ended. The bull won.

A "Dude Friday," the old man said before leaving the apartment for work. Some sort of home care attendant to help out when Kevin needed an extra set of hands—a service his dad made clear he would no longer personally offer. Their insurance covered so many weeks. The rest, dear old dad emoted in one final parting shot, could come out of Kevin's own pocket.

A humid gray day brooded outside, not the best weather but good for any number of young adult male activities should said male have two good working legs. Waylaid on the sofa, about the only way to get through such a day was through masturbation. Kevin dialed down the TV's volume, reached to the coffee table for his tablet, and called up one of his favorite porn videos while trying to banish the last of his father's words and the image attached to them. Friday was Robinson Crusoe's trusted right-hand man, he remembered from reading the book in one of his English classes. And since landing at his father's place, Kevin *had* felt shipwrecked and alone on a tiny, tufted island.

The video showed an attractive dude in an ice hockey uniform, a real man's man, with a prickle of scruff on his square chin and a don't-fuck-with-me expression. Another uniformed dude knelt before him and fished the stud's dick out of his hockey gear—a hairy, uncut beaut. The stud's balls followed. A sloppy, slobbering hum job commenced. Kevin's bone pulsed. For another second or so, he was the hockey jock getting serviced, with Doc Olber as the teammate on his knees. Then they switched roles and Kevin was the skilled cocksucker on his knees providing service. It didn't matter which. He was so fucking horny!

He remembered his father's words—a home health caregiver. An image of sensible nursing shoes formed in his imagination, killing the buzz. A stranger in spectacles helping him to bathe, and acting high and mighty and in total control when he was at his most vulnerable, his most *naked.*

A knock sounded on the front door. Kevin shook himself out of the trance. He waited, sucked in a shallow sip of air. Another repetition shocked him fully out of the spell.

"Shit," he grunted, stopping the video right as the stud began to bust his seed all over his teammate's face. *"Just a sec—!"*

Kevin reached for his crutches. He realized his dick still hung out of his shorts, still stiff, a pearl of pre-cum leaking from its hole. He attempted to stuff his balls back under cover, only to see stars. Grunting another swear, he pivoted on his right foot, ignored the drag of gravity from the left, and maneuvered forward, toward the front door.

The itch surged, somewhere between his knee and his toes. Air licked at his nuts. He made it to the door, balanced his weight, turned the knob.

"Kevin, I presume," a deep male voice asked from outside in the new day's gray murk.

Kevin blinked. The stars burned down. The hot hockey stud from the porn video had jumped out of his tablet and onto the front stoop.

"Yeah?" he managed.

"I'm Andre. I'm your—"

"You're my Dude Friday," said Kevin.

Andre flashed a grin that showed a length of clean white teeth. "Guess you could say that."

He extended his hand, a big one. Kevin accepted the gesture and shook.

Andre wore a powder-blue scrub top over khaki pants with cargo pockets, and decent sneakers on huge feet. While maneuvering away from the door on his crutches, Kevin absorbed the rest of the man's details. Andre was older, but not by too much—mid- to late-twenties, he guessed. His bare arms showed plenty of muscle, hair, even some ink. A scrollwork pattern wound around the dude's biceps.

Square-jawed, a fine prickle of dark scruff was starting to show on his throat, chin, and cheeks. Andre smelled of clean male sweat and a trace of deodorant. Kevin stole a look at the dude's perfect ass on his way into the apartment and was again conscious of his pulsing dick and loose, swinging nuts.

He shut the door. The dude's smile lingered.

"Hoops injury, huh?"

"Sad but true," Kevin said, his voice sounding alien, belonging to somebody else.

Andre sucked in a deep breath. Kevin's dick attempted to jump out of his shorts on its own power, driven back to its full hardness by the knowledge that Andre smelled him, too.

"Sorry, it's a little messy in here, and by mess, I mean me. It's a bit ripe," the stranger in control of his voice apologized.

"A bit?" Andre said, punctuating the comeback with a good-natured chuckle. "Maybe we should start our working relationship by fixing that problem and airing the place out."

Kevin noticed the porn movie, the action paused but still visible on his tablet, but to his surprise a lightness fell over him. Most of what had happened that summer no longer pissed him off. He liked this guy. A lot. "Whatever you say."

"Whatever *I* say? I like that."

Andre knelt between Kevin's spread legs, in the same position as Doctor Olber when the cast went on. Kevin tried to ignore the demands of his dick and the growing looseness of his nuts as the dude wrapped a plastic garbage bag around his cast and secured it in place with surgical tape drawn from one of those cargo pockets.

"We can't risk getting it wet," Andre said.

The dude's voice stoked Kevin's excitement, as did the motion of his fingers over the cast. The sound of running water droned in the background.

"There, now let's get you cleaned up, buddy."

Andre helped him into the bathroom. Kevin stripped off his

shirt and smelled the sweat from his armpits, aware of it in a way he wasn't before Andre's arrival.

"Can you get those on your own or do you need my help?" the dude asked.

Kevin followed Andre's gaze down to his shorts. Without them, he'd be completely bare in front of his new pal. Swallowing, Kevin discovered his mouth had gone completely dry. "Uh," he started, and considered the bigger picture. "I wouldn't say no to some help, dude."

"No sweat," said Andre, though that wasn't exactly true.

Andre took hold of Kevin's shorts at the waistband and tugged. Kevin's shorts lowered down, down. A breathless moment later, they were at his knees. His dick snapped up, fully erect, while his stones plummeted, and only his hairy sac kept them from rolling across the linoleum.

"Hello," Andre growled.

His shorts reached his ankles and Kevin stepped out of them with his Dude Friday's help. "Sorry."

"Don't be," Andre said. "I saw what was on your screen. I figured I must have showed at your door while you were in the middle of rubbing one out. We've all been there. And I bet this isn't the first time you've thrown wood around your buddies in the locker room, right?"

Kevin's stomach attempted to follow his nuts onto the bathroom floor. "Sure," he said, laughing.

Their eyes connected, and Kevin's bone throbbed. Dare he think it? Was the dude as excited by the unfolding scenario taking place between a pair of strangers? He saw Andre's throat knot. The chemical spark between them was real.

"OK, let's do this," Andre said.

Then he removed his scrub shirt. The bare torso beneath was as magnificent as Kevin suspected, dusted in dark hair across the pecs, with plenty of fur showing above the waistband of the dude's underwear, which protruded above his belt.

Andre wrapped an arm around Kevin's back. "Easy. Easy …"

Kevin attempted to focus, which proved nearly impossible after he caught Andre's eyes staring at his dick. The dude helped him into the tub. Kevin eased into the hot water, with his left leg, the cast wrapped in plastic, hanging over the edge. Andre handed him a washcloth and the bar of soap.

"Do what you can," the dude said. "I'll get the rest."

In a daze, Kevin soaped up his chest and both pits. From there, under Andre's watchful eyes, he washed lower, lathering up the thatch of curls around his erection. He grabbed his nuts with one hand and his dick in the other. The pent-up energy that had tormented him for days crackled, consuming his entire body in electrical pulses. Kevin's skin tingled with pins and needles as Andre knelt beside the tub, ready to help out.

"Nice," the other man said.

Andre reached between his legs for the abandoned bar of soap. Kevin gasped, driven almost to the verge of unloading by the brush of the other man's fingertips over his sac. The fucking tease of it—a second after making contact, Andre stood and leaned over the tub. He took Kevin's bare right foot and caressed it with soap from ankle to toes. Energy surged up Kevin's leg. His cock tried to jump out of his hand. A moan flew past his lips before he could trap it.

"Like that?"

Kevin nodded. "Fuck yeah, I like it."

Andre's soapy hands worked higher, past ankle to hairy calf. A shudder attempted to hurl its way down Kevin's spine. He fought it, failed. Cold and hot battled for control of his flesh.

Higher, his new Dude Friday's fingers walked up to his knee. Andre again crouched beside the tub. Their eyes met.

103

"How am I doing?" asked Andre.

"You fucking make me feel so much better," Kevin confessed.

"That's what I was hired for," Andre said. "An extra set of hands to help you out until you're back on both feet."

Suddenly, breathing was no longer easy or even involuntary. Kevin waited, the pressure pushing on his chest.

"Extra set of fingers," Andre repeated, and grabbed hold of Kevin's dick.

Kevin moaned, tensed, and then imagined that the rest of his bones had dissolved around the heat in the dude's grip. A picture formed, that of his body as loose and liquid as his nuts, the only prevailing stiffness in his cock. Andre stroked him up and down with a tightening choke hold.

"Dude," Kevin sighed.

"This OK?"

Kevin focused on the other man, so handsome, so helpful. "It's fucking great—jerk my dick, dude!"

Andre did. At one point, he leaned closer, and all Kevin could think about was kissing him. As though sensing this as any great assistant would, Andre met him halfway. Their mouths crushed together awkwardly. Lips aligned. Andre groaned, the vibrations deep and guttural. Kevin tested the dude's willingness with the tip of his tongue. Andre accepted his offer, and their tongues looped while the dude jerked him faster, harder.

It wouldn't take long, Kevin sensed. Heat boiled in his nuts. Boldly, he reached his left hand past the tub and between Andre's legs, finding the dude's dick as hard as he hoped. He squeezed the other man's thickness. Andre huffed into his mouth, indicating approval. Their tongues released.

"I'm gonna like looking after you," Andre said. "Making sure you get the best care. Everything you need."

Kevin's skeletal system reformed as his body tensed in the tub. He was boned-up everywhere now, a young man made entirely of cock. "I'm gonna bust, dude!"

Andre's mouth joined his fingers, and the dude sucked Kevin's dick down, almost to the nuts. Kevin's balls unloaded what felt like a gallon of whitewash. He was still squirting when Andre pulled back. Seed splashed the dude's chin before their mouths again locked. They kissed, and Kevin feasted on the taste of his own wad.

The dude started to pull away. Kevin drew him back by his dick. "Wait …"

Andre's smirk returned. "I have to do my job, need to get you cleaned up."

Kevin's fingers squeezed Andre's thickness through his pants. "Let's get dirty some more first."

Andre stood, yanked on his zipper, and unbuckled his belt. Kevin shifted, aware of the itch again, the elf, the whole cruel way the summer had played out. Only as he took his first taste of Andre's cock, none of it troubled him. The itch would get scratched, and he didn't feel like a man alone on a deserted island with only his dick to keep him company anymore.

MEAT LOVERS
Natty Soltesz

I was hungry but I didn't know what for. My wife had left that morning with our baby to visit her mother for the weekend. I'd spent most of the morning laying around, feeling guilty for not going with her. We'd fought about it. I texted her, she didn't text back. I played some video games. I went outside; it was a hot summer day. I looked over the wall that enclosed my yard and saw someone a few yards down, puttering around, a neighbor I didn't know.

Here was I was, twenty-seven years old, in the house we'd just bought six months ago, and I felt like a bored teenager. I wished I had some pot, which was weird—I'd smoked only a couple times in college, never since then. I wanted something, anything. I wanted to be a little bad.

So, I ordered a pizza. It was something my wife wouldn't abide by. She had a moratorium on all junk food in the house. I got anchovies, pepperoni, and olives, and they said it'd be there in forty-five minutes.

I thought about watching TV. I thought about taking my TV into the backyard and smashing it with a sledgehammer. I got a beer out of the fridge and sucked it down in ten minutes. Then I had another.

I was on my third beer when I got the idea to put some music on—The White Stripes, which was exactly right. I was walking down the hall when I caught a look at myself in the mirror. It made me stop and set down my beer. I was wearing a pair of athletic shorts and a T-shirt with the sleeves cut off. I lifted up the shirt.

I'm hot, was what I was thinking. In fact I sort of looked hotter than I ever have. My black hair was still thick, my jaw strong. My body had thickened but even that looked good, my abs nice and defined with a brush of dark hair over them, hair that became denser as it led into the waistband of my shorts.

I realized I was getting turned on just from looking at myself. It brought back memories of being a horny teenager when all I'd have to do was think about my dick and it would start to get hard. I felt like I hadn't noticed myself in years. When I jacked off, I'd do it before Angela came to bed or in the shower, quick and fast, my eyes closed—a duty to be done. Our sex life was normal, but that was done in the dark, too—and truthfully, things had slacked off considerably since Maggie was born.

I ran my hand up my hairy, muscled chest, then back down my stomach and let my fingers dip into my waistband. I wanted to see *all* of me, because I was pretty sure my cock still looked as good as it had when I was younger.

I was starting to pull down the waistband when the doorbell rang.

Fuck. I had a full boner and now I had to go answer the door. I took some deep breaths and tried to will my cock to soften. It didn't go down much so I tucked it under the waistband and hoped for the best.

What would be the harm in showing off a little, anyway? I thought. I opened the door and there he stood. The pizza guy.

"Hey," he said, nodding his head at me. I'd ordered a large but because the minimum for delivery was fifteen bucks I got a two-liter as well, so both of his hands were full. He was young—twenty-one, if that—with sandy blond hair that curled out from under his baseball cap. He had blond stubble on his square chin and little black spacers in his earlobes. He was in his prime, I suppose, while I was past mine, but you could tell he was wasting it a little, reveling a little too hard in his youth, probably getting fucked up most nights on cheap canned beer and dirt weed. Still, his body was fit and toned under his flour-caked red T-shirt and sort-of-black, kitchen-filthy pants, his posture easy and available.

"It's fifteen fifty," he said. My cock was still tucked back under my waistband but it had softened. I casually let it drop and he didn't seem to notice. I reached for my pocket before I realized I didn't have one.

"Shoot—it's inside." When he shifted on his feet, the unglued sole of his ratty black Converse fell open like a mouth. "Hold on a moment ..."

"Actually," he said, putting his foot back flat and leaning just slightly in as if to look past me and into the house. "Can I use your bathroom?"

"Sure. Absolutely," I said, opening the door wide and stepping aside. "There's one right down the hall."

"Thanks, man," he said, and stepped past me. He stood there for a moment, awkwardly holding the pizza and soda until I took it from him. I pointed the way and he headed down the hall and into the bathroom. He swung the door behind him but it didn't shut—I was used to this. It bounced back and stayed half-open. The pizza guy didn't try to close it, which seemed strange.

I stood there for a moment as the sound of piss burbling into the toilet came to me, heavy and low. I couldn't remember where my wallet was. Why was I getting so distracted? It was my horn-iness, I realized. It had just crept up on me. There was some-thing about this young guy, something that registered on a deep part of my brain that I wasn't used to hearing from. Something sexy ...

I was just standing there with the food in my hands. I remem-bered that my wallet was on the kitchen counter. I headed down the hall, the sound of the pizza guy's piss getting a little less robust—he was finishing up. I intended to go quickly past him, to keep my gaze forward, to keep it normal.

When I got to the open door, though, I couldn't stop myself. I glanced inside. I intended it to be just that—glance once then look away—but what I saw so surprised me that I stopped in my tracks.

He was turned away from me but I could just see the front of him, and he was shaking off his cock into the toilet. His cock was huge. It hung low and was beer-can thick. It was sort of impossible to ignore.

He had a hand on the waistband of his underwear, the other hand holding up his jeans, and he was just tucking it inside his underwear when he looked up and our eyes met. It was just a moment, a glance, but my anxiety caught in my throat. I quickly looked away and walked on. The look on his face was inscrutable at that moment—not a rebuke, but not an invitation, either. It was too quick to process.

I set down the pizza and soda and got the money out of my wal-let. I was counting it out when he walked into the kitchen. I stole another glance at his crotch, I think—I wanted to know where he was keeping that thing, how it fit in there. He did have a sizeable bulge, it even looked a little swollen, like the root of it was getting larger and making a dome-like tent in his zipper area. I handed him a twenty and a single. "Here you go," I said.

He took the money without a word and tucked it into the front right pocket of his pants. Then he looked at me, a level, serious look that made my heart quicken. He moved his eyes to my still-open wallet.

"You want anything else?" he asked.

I didn't know what to say, even if a part of me knew what he was suggesting.

"I'll let you see it for that ten," he said, nodding toward my wallet. "But you can touch it for twenty."

I wanted to see it. Something about this young man's brash confidence, his *cockiness,* was intoxicating. I reached in my wallet and took out the ten. He snatched it out of my hand and made as if to shove it in his front pocket, but stopped.

"You sure you don't want to touch it?" he asked, in an almost accusing way, like he'd been down this road before and *everybody* ended up wanting to touch it. "'Cause once I take it out, you can't change your mind." I bit my lip. "I'll let you look for a minute but if you try to touch it I'll fuck you up. Better give me that other ten now."

I dipped back into my wallet and pulled out the other ten dollar bill. The kid's cockeyed grin was somehow obnoxious and sexy at the same time.

He took the other bill and stuffed both into his pants. Then, without looking up, he began to unbutton them. "You got a minute and a half," he said. He looked at me. "Got it?"

"OK," I said, nodding. I was outside my body; I'd entered some other world, where the roles were switched and I was being held sway by this sexy little punk of a pizza boy.

"Don't try to kiss it or anything queer like that," he said as he reached into his underwear. He took hold, lifted, and there it was, hanging like a fire hose half-engorged and thickening. He let it hang there outside his pants. He flexed it and it bounced just a little, quavering like a ripple atop a lake.

I stared in awe and, well, confusion. I was surprised at myself. Of course I'd always had fantasies about playing with another guy's dick—any guy who says he hasn't wondered about it is lying, or very out of touch with his sexuality. I mean, most straight porn is half-pussy, half-schlong anyway. You have to wonder.

But fantasizing about something and actually doing it are two different things, of course. I found myself wishing I hadn't paid to touch it after all, that if I'd kept it just as a look it would be safer somehow. Here was this ginormous cock held out for me to play with—it was a little intimidating, I suppose.

And it kept getting more intimidating, engorging and rising as we stood there in the kitchen, the clock ticking, the refrigerator droning its anxious hum. "Time's wasting, buddy," he said, and just the way he said "buddy" had the drip of domination about it. This kid may have been younger than me but he knew exactly what I wanted and exactly what he'd let me do, nothing more. "I got two more deliveries after this. Shit's getting cold."

It hung nearly nine inches long and it was so thick that it appeared to be at full erection, even though it wasn't rising up to a ninety-degree angle. What would it feel like in my hand? It was so big …

I reached out and slipped my fingertips underneath it and along the underside until it rested in my palm. I felt its weight, its heat. I pulled my hand forward and felt it drag against my palm. It got harder. I wrapped my fingers around the plum-like head, round and solid, and gently squeezed it. His shaft just continued to expand, the core of it girded with a steel tension rod, spongy tissue, hot and engorged, filling it out, puffy veins thick as pipes curling around it.

I stroked it, from the tip down to the base. My hand could barely close around the base. The stroke made him shift on his feet a little. I looked up at his face. He was looking right at me; some of the cockiness had dissipated.

"Damn, bro," he said, looking down at me. "You got me so hard." I pulled my palm back up. It twitched a little, and the head bounced up. "Didn't realize I was so horny."

I leaned my face into it. I wasn't even aware I was doing it—I just wanted to get closer to it, its heat, to feel it against my arm, my face, my lips. Then without realizing it I was getting on my knees. He responded by backing away and swiping my hand away from his cock.

"I shoulda figured you'd try that," he said, smirking.

"I won't suck it," I said.

"Better not," he said, and relaxed his stance. I held it again, wrapping my fist around it this time. My fingers barely closed around it. I jacked it once, twice.

"Minute's almost up," he said. I tried to smell him without making it obvious. It was musky, yeasty, like sweat and weed and pizza dough. He noticed instantly. "Like sniffin' my dong?" he asked, laughing. "My sweaty nards?" I sniffed down toward them. It sounds crazy but they smelled even better. It was a familiar smell, of course, one I sort of appreciated on myself even if I was aware that it didn't smell "good," particularly. But smelling him was different.

"Queers, man," he said, laughing. "Alright, I'll let you lick those. Since you like the smell so much. But just my nuts, nothing else alright? Alright?"

"Yes," I said. I got down lower. Was I ready for this? I took a good sniff of his balls, pressing my nose now into his nest of damp sandy-brown pubes. I took a good whiff and my cock just throbbed. The smell was so different from a woman, but so familiar to me that it had this disorienting effect that revved my libido into a vortex. I put out my tongue and licked up under them, letting the left one roll on my tongue just a bit. I wanted more of that smell. I wanted it to cover me.

"I'll let you kiss it, then," he said, and now I could tell he was really turned on, maybe as much as I was. "Just a kiss, though, cause I'm so fuckin horny."

I let the tip of his cock graze my nose. There was slickness at the tip, in the slit—not quite a drop, but a stickiness that made the head of his cock stick to my nose for just a second before it jerked and popped upward. I put my lips to it, feeling the heat of it on my lips. I put my lips to it and kissed, just as sweet and soft as could be.

"Nice," he said. "Kiss it again." I gently kissed the head, the slit. I kept kissing, down the sticky skin of his shaft, smacking my lips against his hot flesh, loving, worshipful kisses to show him how much I appreciated his beautiful cock, how unworthy I was to be kissing such a piece, how grateful. "Fuck yes," he said. When I got to his nuts I kissed them, then made my way back up, smooch smooch smooch until I was kissing the head. This time there was a solid drop of pre-cum there.

"If you lick it, it's going to go in your ass," I heard him saying, but my mind wasn't quite paying attention. I was focused on that drop of pre-cum, and I put my lips to it so that it smeared into my lips. *Smooch.* His breath was getting ragged. I was rock hard in my shorts. "Got that? Lick it if you want but don't start what you can't finish. I don't go for just blow jobs—if you get me going and I need to fuck, it's going in your ass. Understand?" The slit of his cock was wide and fat, almost like a little cunt, and I never stopped, it just happened—I brought out my tongue and licked into it, into the tiny pool of his pre-jizz, the hot slit of his giant cock. It tasted so

113

good, tasted like me, tasted like a juicy cock. He let out his breath. "You've done it now," he said as I went in for another lick, instantly resigned to my fate. He took me by the chin. "You know what you're in for, right?" he asked. All I could do was nod. He put his cock back in my face. I honestly had never been fucked and had no idea if I could get fucked, let alone take a piece as massive as his. However, as soon as I thought that I felt my hole loosen and get hot, like it was hungry, begging with its mouth open.

I licked up his shaft, licking it fully this time, my tongue flat and wide, tasting as much of him as I could, getting every inch of the underside wet with my spit. It tasted so good, young salty horny flesh.

"Fuck yes," he said, letting out his breath. "You know that you want that cock inside you, filling up your hot little faggot ass. Don't you?"

It was funny that he called me faggot given that I'd never even touched another guy's cock up until that moment, but he really sold the whole macho thing. Anyway I didn't answer 'cause I didn't know for sure if I wanted it or not. Instead I took the head of it into my mouth and wrapped my tongue around it, suckling it like it was a plum I was about to bite into. All I knew was that I wanted to stuff as much of that piece into my puss as I could. I let the head pass over my tongue, let it poke into my mouth. My throat muscles relaxed as my ass muscles relaxed. It wasn't just curiosity about a big cock that had gotten me to where I was at that moment, it was that what he was saying was true: I wanted it *inside* me. My lips stretched around it, my throat felt like I'd swallowed five hot dogs at the same time, my eyes were watering and my nose wasn't even touching his pubic hair yet. I had to come up and get a breath.

"C'mon cocksucker, you can do better than that," he said. I tried again, starting at the tip and working my mouth and throat down it.

114

My throat felt like it stretched out a little more this time. Feeling my face get filled up by that massive schlong was an intoxicating thing. I imagined what it was like for my wife, imagined I was her, and that's when I moved my hand down my back and into my shorts so I could feel my hole, press my fingers into its heat. Yeah, I wanted to be a whore for him. I wanted to be his fuck hole, to be used.

But wanting is one thing and getting is another. When he impatiently pulled his cock out of my mouth I knew I was due for the latter and I got a little scared.

"Ready to get your guts rammed in?" he asked.

"I don't know …" I said, standing and wiping my mouth.

"Fuck you don't," he said, standing there with his pants around his ankles. He pulled off his shirt, knocking his cap to the floor in the process, and stood there mostly naked, stroking his cock in front of him. He had a flat, sexy stomach, the slightest definition of pectorals on his chest, no hair anywhere but for right above his cock. He took my arm and spun me around so that I was facing the counter.

"Tell me you've never had a cock up your ass before," he said.

"Never."

"A virgin?" he said, and pushed his hand against my lower back so that my torso lowered and I had to brace myself against the counter. I heard what sounded like him wetting his finger in his mouth, then he pressed it to my ass, fumbling a bit to find my hole. When he found it he shoved his finger in, just like that. The shock of it made me jerk forward but he didn't seem to notice or care. He pushed his finger in once, twice. "Fucking A. I love virgins. Tight as hell." I concentrated on breathing and relaxing and was surprised to find that it was pretty enjoyable.

"Please go easy on me," I said. He just laughed and took out his finger.

"I'll lube you up, that's about it. Got any slippery stuff? Vaseline? Crisco?" I went to the cabinet and grabbed the first thing I found— a bottle of my wife's expensive olive oil. Extra virgin.

"Alright," he said as I handed to him. He threw the cap on the floor, poured some on his cock and smoothed it all over, then brought two oily fingers to my hole and shoved them in just as unceremoniously as he'd slid in the first one. I might have gasped a little but, again, after I got over the shock of the invasion it felt good. Even better than just one.

"Fuck, I need to cum," he said, and took out his fingers. He pressed the head of his cock against my ass and I took a deep breath and did my best to prepare myself. He pushed down on my back again so that my ass would be more perfectly perched up for him. I think that was the best part of it for me, the way he seemed fully focused on his own pleasure and willing to use me for it, like I was just a tight place to deposit his seed, something a little better than his hand but not worth much else.

When the head of his massive schlong popped inside I nearly cried out, but I think I was too shocked to do that. Then I was just trying to catch my breath because he was not giving me any time to adjust—he just kept pushing it in at a steady clip, inch by inch, groaning as if savoring the tightness of my tight virgin asshole.

"Goddamn that's good," he said and he bottomed out, his pubes and nuts pushed against me. My face was covered in sweat and I felt like I had a torpedo lodged in my guts, but otherwise I was fine. When he pulled out and shoved it back in I found it intensely pleasurable, not just because I was making good use of myself as a sheath for his cock but because he was tripping a switch in me— the prostate, I suppose.

"Take that cock you fucking slut," he said, grabbing onto my hips and banging me from behind, steady quick thrusts that made

116

his nuts slap against me, the sound of skin hitting skin and our moans echoing in the quiet of the kitchen. I wondered if this was how my wife would like to get fucked. I tended to treat girls delicately, focused on their pleasure, on getting them off. I'd never been like this.

Mostly I was holding on for dear life, so it was a surprise when I reached down to feel my cock and realized I was mostly hard. In fact I'd dripped so much that there was a little trail of pre-cum from where my cock was riding against the side of the counter. I held on to my cock and stroked while he banged me, his thrusts getting wilder and rougher, slamming his pelvis so hard against me that it hurt.

"Fuck I'm gonna shoot in you soon. Ready to take my load?"

"Uh-huh," I said. I felt like I was getting ready to cum myself, one hand pressed into the granite countertop, as he battered against me, my other hand stroking my cock.

"Ready to get bred? You fucking slut. Take it. Oh fuck!" With a single mighty thrust, he slammed his whole cock into my hole, his drawn-up nuts pulsing as he emptied them inside me. Shot after shot of his load flooded my guts.

I came at the same time, my load splattering against the counter. It was one of the best orgasms I ever had.

He pulled out.

"Fuck I'm late," he said, pulling up his pants. I looked back to see his cock, now reduced in size, dripping and slick. I pulled up my shorts. What the hell had just happened? "Guess you got your money's worth."

"Thank you," I said. He just smirked, then turned and went out the door. I felt his load dripping out of my hole and down my thighs. I opened the box, the pizza was still warm. I grabbed a slice and took a big bite, and when I needed a drink I chugged the soda right from the bottle.

CLEAN HOUSE, DIRTY MIND
P.A. Friday

I won't lie: When I organized getting a cleaner, I expected it to be a woman. The manager of the company, Jodi, was a middle-aged woman who was scarily organized and probably knew as much as I did about my house by the end of our conversation.

"Right," she said briskly, "I'll send Alex round twice a week for a couple of hours. Tuesdays at three and Fridays at nine."

"Yes. Thanks," I said weakly. While the idea of being awake at nine on a Friday morning horrified me—hey, I'm a freelance photographer; I don't keep office hours—you'd have had to be a stronger willed person than me to argue with Jodi—and she was out the door before I could even say good-bye.

As I say, Jodi was middle-height, middle-aged, and wearing a suit which suggested she didn't do much of the actual cleaning these days. I imagined Alex as a small thin woman, probably as organized as Jodi, who would take one look at the cluttered shabbiness I called home and suck her teeth disapprovingly. I looked thoughtfully at some of the photos I had on the wall—nude studies, if you want the pretentious version; naked hot guys, if you prefer to be blunt—and wondered whether I ought to take them down. There was nothing pornographic about them, but some people get funny about that sort of thing. In the end, I decided to leave them—I couldn't be up and down with them twice a week to spare the sensibilities of some woman who was, after all, getting paid to be there.

Of course, by Tuesday, I'd forgotten all about the cleaner coming. I'd given Jodi a key for Alex to use because freelancing meant I never knew where I was going to be at any point of the day. So I was happily scanning through the latest batch of pictures—photos for the soft end of the porn industry—when the door opened.

Unfortunately, I was getting hard from what I was looking at and happened to be rubbing a hand in the area of my crotch.

I swore under my breath, suddenly remembering that this was the first day of Project House-Clean. I fumbled with the mouse, trying to click off the pictures, but there was no denying what had been there. I could only hope my new cleaning woman wasn't some straight-lace who'd be out of my house before we'd even said hello. A voice came from behind me.

"Hello," it said, relieving me of one of my worries, but raising another.

I turned my head to discover I was looking at a bloke. A tall, dark, smoking-hot hunk of a man. Oh, Christ. When your first sight of a new client is him looking at explicit photos with a hard-on that's threatening to break the placket of his trousers, what are you supposed to think?

"Hi," I mumbled back.

"I'm Alex."

"I gathered." I stood up and wiped sweaty hands down my trousers, immediately realizing this could be taken the wrong way. "Er … Matt. Freelance photographer." I stuck out my arm and we shook hands awkwardly. How bloody British. "I … sorry, I'd forgotten that you were… I was just …" (don't go there) "working. And I thought you'd be …" (don't go there, either). I trailed off.

"Female," Alex said, with a resigned half-smile. "I can clean, I promise. Is there anything in particular you want me to do?"

"No, no. Just—clean," I said. "I'll get on with …" I flapped a hand at my computer and saw a faint pink color tinge Alex's face. Bugger. He'd seen them. "On second thought, I've got a bit of shopping to do. I'll nip down to Morrisons."

"I'll get on." Alex backed out of the room and closed the door, and by the time I left the house five minutes later (computer safely shut down), he was well away with a cloth and cleaning fluid.

I didn't return until I was certain he'd have left.

There's nothing like a stag "do" to lower your defenses. I'd been hired to take candid shots of a groom-to-be and his mates in the early hours of the evening—but I did it too well and they asked me to join them for the rest of the night. The best man was giving me a bit of a come-on and he wasn't half bad-looking, so I went. And despite the fact that all I got out of him was a snog, it would have been a good night were it not a Thursday evening … and a particularly late one at that …

So yeah. I was dead to the world on Friday morning when the door to my room suddenly banged open and I heard this vaguely familiar voice go:

"Oh God, sorry."

"Fuck." I blinked blurrily at Alex, who'd first met me with a hard-on and now had a viewing of *all* of my wares as I was spread naked over the duvet cover. "I mean—sorry, I'll be dressed in a mo. I kind of forgot it was—" I tried to remember what day we'd agreed Alex would come at this god-awful time of morning—

120

But Alex had already backed out again. I couldn't blame him. I heard his voice from the other side of the door. "Not a problem. I'll, um, just start elsewhere."

I rubbed the sleep from my eyes and, swearing under my breath, grabbed a robe and shrugged myself into it before heading for the bathroom. A hot shower later, I was at least capable of pretending to be human. Trouble was, I needed (and I mean *needed*) a coffee. Which brought up a whole new problem. What was the etiquette around drinks for your cleaner? I'd left some stuff out so that Alex could help himself if he wanted to, but it seemed kind of rude to barge into the kitchen and make myself a drink without offering him something. Deciding I'd rather be seen as overly polite and interfering than rude, I decided to ask Alex if he wanted a drink. He was humming under his breath as he worked; something cheerful-sounding that I didn't know.

"Um, hi … Did you want a drink? I've just boiled the kettle." It was the first sensible thing I'd actually said to the guy.

He turned, startled, the humming stopping as he realized I'd heard him. "Oh, thanks. Yes, please."

"How do you like it?" Fuck, why did everything sound like an innuendo when I talked to Alex?

"Oh, just black."

When the drinks were ready, we sat at the kitchen table and I tried to make conversation that would demonstrate I was a normal human being and not some sex-obsessed weirdo. Which, of course, made it almost impossible to think of anything to say that couldn't be taken the wrong way. In the end, I was painfully British.

"Nicer day today."

Alex slurped his coffee. I wondered whether he was trying to

121

neck it down at twice the speed to get away from me. "Yeah. I thought it was supposed to chuck it down with rain."

"There's still time," I said wryly, and he smiled.

After that, it became a bit of a routine. If I was home, I'd make us both a coffee and we'd sit in the kitchen for ten minutes or so as we drank them. At first, Alex tried valiantly to make up the "wasted" time at the end of his session, but after I'd packed him off home for the sixth time he relaxed and realized I meant it.

But there was an on-going problem with having Alex cleaning my house, and that was that he was drop-dead gorgeous and, not to put too fine a point on it, I was in lust. As in, rock-hard, middle-of-the-night wankfest lust. It was sometimes even difficult to meet his eyes across the kitchen table when I remembered what I'd had him doing in my mind the night before.

And a couple of months in, Alex made it just that much more difficult. "Did you take those photos?" he asked suddenly, out of nowhere.

I instantly remembered my first concern when getting a cleaner, and wondered again whether I should have taken them down. "Yes. Is it a problem?"

"No, no," he said hastily. "I just …"

I waited for him to finish but he said no more, so I lifted the coffee to my lips and took another gulp.

"Would you photograph me?"

I choked on a mouthful of hot coffee. "What?"

"Nothing."

"You mean," I said slowly, "like the ones I have up? The nudes?"

"It was a stupid idea." Alex was backing up quickly and blushing a fiery red.

"No, not at all." I looked at him appraisingly—all in the name of Art, obviously. "I could do that."

"I'd pay you," he assured me.

Which was good, don't get me wrong—you don't want to know how many people think freelance has an emphasis on the *free*—but at the same time, I didn't want Alex feeling like I'd been judging his financial status.

"Or," I suggested, "we could do a quid pro quo—you do some additional jobs, like cleaning out the kitchen cupboards—" (which I hadn't dared open for months after stuffing them to the bursting point with God-knows-what) "—and I'll take photos."

"Oh, not at the same time, surely?" Alex protested with a bit of a grin.

I laughed, trying not to dwell on how much I could get off on the thought of Alex crawling round my kitchen in the buff. "No, we can do it at your place, whenever." I quite liked the thought of getting a gander at his house, considering he knew so much about mine.

His face fell. "Couldn't we do it here?" he asked. "I'm in a flat share, and …" He trailed off.

I'd made the rule when I first started up, never to work in my home. At least, never to have clients here. I knew a studio I could go to if necessary, but it hiked the prices up quite a lot, and if Alex was flat-sharing, it didn't sound like he was exactly flush. And I couldn't insist on him cleaning every cupboard in my fricking house in order to earn the pictures. Plus, he was gorgeous and I'd practically pay to see him naked.

I conveniently forgot the rule. "Yeah, OK. We could do that …"

I should have known it was a bad idea. Yet ten days later, with my kitchen cupboards newly sparkling and arranged to within an inch of their lives, I had Alex, naked, in my bedroom. Or, to be strictly accurate, I didn't "have" him, which was the problem.

I'm a professional. I can always turn my mind off during a job and concentrate solely on the photos. Except, it turned out, when a guy I'd been wanking over for weeks was sprawled across my bed in a way that showed me without a doubt that my fantasies had been a pale imitation of reality. Had I thought him hot the first moment I'd seen him? I'd been wrong. He was way, way above that, and my cock knew it.

"OK," I said, trying to sound briskly professional, but grateful for the camera paraphernalia with which I could hide my erection. "Do you have any preferences about positions, or …" My cock did a little waggle to tell me that it could think of any number of positions to put Alex in, most of them involving me doing him hard and fast up the arse. I shifted uncomfortably. "I mean, for the pictures," I added hastily.

Then I felt like an idiot, because what else was he going to think I was talking about? It wasn't like he knew I was standing here perving over him. The photos round the house were explicit but not specifically sexual. I mean, you could probably get an idea of my orientation from the fact that I had pictures of naked men on my walls but that was the extent of it. And my professional reputation was something I was actually quite proud of: not the slightest taint of scandal. My private and professional lives were kept absolutely separate, and that was the way I liked it.

I suddenly realized that Alex had said something I'd totally missed, my mind busy on its own train of thought.

"Sorry, wool-gathering," I apologized—an expression of my grandmother's which I'd never had reason to use before.

"Sorry," said Alex, like it was his fault. "I … um …" He grinned. There ought to be laws against Alex grinning unexpectedly. "It feels a bit weird taking my clothes off in front of a guy I'm not sleeping with." My gaydar pricked up its antenna—was Alex implying he was gay? I'd presumed that the photos were intended for—well, women. Most male models were aiming for the feminine market, in my experience. "So if you can give me a few secs to get used to you behind a camera …"

"Sure. You get comfortable, and I'll just—" I flapped a hand vaguely at the door "—go and get some things." Yeah.

OK, so I was copping out. Running away. But my cock was going to explode if I stayed there any longer watching Alex wriggle about all over my bed. I shut the door a bit harder than I intended and headed for the bathroom, locking it behind me. Then—God, the relief—I unzipped my trousers and let my painfully hard cock spring free. I might have given a little moan as I gripped myself firmly and began to stroke.

Alex. Fuck, Alex, naked on my bed. Those muscles. That arse. That slender cock. I imagined what it would feel like to run my hand down his prick, as I did it to my own. His was longer, but thinner. Would he give that little grin as I began to wank him? How long would it take before he asked me to fuck him? My hand slid faster and faster and I was having trouble breathing. Would he lie on his back, spread his legs apart for me? Or would I have him on all fours, doggy style, my hand still curved around him, wanking him good and hard as I pounded into his arse? I didn't last long; seconds later I shot my load before leaning a damp forehead against the tiled wall. Fuck. How inappropriate was this, jerking off in the toilet while Alex was naked in the next room, expecting a professional photographer to be—well, professional?

I cleaned myself up as hastily as I could and splashed cold water over my face for good measure. I could do this. It wasn't like it was going to be hard … *tough* … to take decent photographs of Alex. He was every photographer's dream—rather too literally in my case.

"Bathroom break," I said briefly when I came back.

"I thought you went for some equipment," Alex said, confused.

Had I said that? "Malfunction of my own equipment," I replied, trying to make a joke out of something which was actually the honest-to-goodness truth. "So, are you getting used to the whole—uh, naked thing?"

"I guess so." Alex shifted awkwardly.

He was half-hard, I noticed with appreciation. A second later, so was I, which I didn't appreciate so much. For God's sake, that wank was supposed to stop this from happening. I wasn't eighteen anymore; my libido was meant to take a while to recover.

My libido had never been faced with Alex before, however.

"OK," I said briskly, trying to sound matter of fact. "So, maybe if we just start with you lying across the bed? Head down here, and then lying on your front."

I indicated what I meant. It was a fairly "safe" posture: no genitalia on show, or anything like that. Hopefully that would help Alex—and me—settle down a bit. Alex followed my instructions to the letter. I concentrated hard on angles and lighting, and *not* on the fact that leaving more to the imagination was just making my imagination work overtime, fue as it now was with some knowledge of what it was that *wasn't* on show. I set up the tripod and then clicked a few frames off.

"Head this way ... Yeah, like that. Now resting on one arm ..."

Alex posed patiently. He was clearly a bit shy about the whole thing, but he could get away with it. Hell, he could get away with anything. It was physically painful to stand behind the camera and pretend my body wasn't responding, that my mind wasn't going through a dozen fantasies a second, each one dirtier than the last.

"Right," I said, my voice hoarse. I coughed. "Sorry. OK, now we've warmed up a bit," (or overheated in my case) "how about a few more explicit shots?"

"Thought you'd never ask," said Alex, stretching lazily and giving me far too good a view of his muscular physique. "Like what?"

Come on, I told myself crossly, I'd done this hundreds of times before. He was just a client. Just another model. "Um," I said eloquently, following it up with "Uh … sit up against the end of the bed."

Oh God, this was hopeless. Grimly, I tried to ignore the increasing pressure from my cock to take notice of it. I wasn't supposed to be thinking about how much I'd like to bone the model. The quick wank earlier hadn't solved anything, just concentrated my mind on how much I wanted him.

"Is this OK?" Alex asked, grinning up at me as he posed naked where I usually slept, leaning up against the wooden bedhead, his crown jewels displayed on the pillow he was sitting on. Which was also the pillow I put my head on every night. If I were there now, his cock would be half inside my mouth from that position.

Damn it. Damn him. Too bloody gorgeous.

"I'm sorry," I muttered, looking everywhere but at Alex. "But I can't … it's not …" I stumbled to a halt, watching Alex's face change from excitement to disappointment.

"I'm not the right type, am I?" Alex said, a grimace on his face. "It's OK, I should have known this wasn't my sort of thing. I did, really, but—"

"It's not you," I interrupted. "It's me. I … if you get the right photographer, you'll be amazing. A star."

"I've heard 'it's not you, it's me' before." Alex pulled his underpants on. "It's never a good conversation. You're a professional photographer—if you can't make me look like anything, I don't reckon anyone else can."

He leaned down to pick up his shirt, but I had somehow taken a step forward, and my foot was on it. "It's not like that." God, this was even more excruciating than I'd anticipated. "Look …" I looked away from him, not able to meet his eye, "I can't take these photos because I'm too … uh … involved."

"Oh, right." I didn't have to be looking at Alex to hear the sarcasm in his voice. "A conflict of interests when your model also happens to be your cleaner. I can see how that might make a difference."

"Fuck it!" I grabbed his arm and pulled his hand against my groin. Even in the less-than-perfect circumstances it felt fucking amazing. "I can't photograph you," I said with grim explicitness, "because I'm too busy thinking about how much I want to fuck you. Conflict of interest? Yeah, how the bloody hell am I supposed to concentrate on angles and lighting when what I really want is my cock up your arse and you sweaty and eager underneath me?"

Well, that had done it. I'd probably lost my cleaner as well as the hottest guy ever to enter my vicinity. It wasn't like Alex was going to feel comfortable cleaning my room when he knew I'd spent half the weekend perving over him. I was still trying not to catch his eye, but I could see the pink spreading across his face. I realized I still had his hand pressed into my crotch, and I let go hastily, stepping away.

"Say that again," Alex said slowly, leaning forward to put his hand back against my frustrated clothes-bound cock.

"God, Alex, you can't not know how bloody gorgeous you are," I grumbled, wondering vaguely whether I'd put too many "nos" and "nots" in that sentence, though most of my concentration was taken up with the fact that Alex was now rubbing his hand up and down, and my cock was thinking *too much* and *not enough* simultaneously.

"So if I were to …"

His hands reached up a bit further and unzipped my trousers. I shrugged my way out of them as fast as I bloody well could. He pulled me over to him, and there was a look in his eyes that would have made the most amazing photograph, except that I was currently a bit distracted by the fact that I was half-naked with the gorgeous bloke I'd been fantasizing about and that—oh fuck—he'd just leaned forwards and taken my cock into his mouth and God-oh-God he was *good* at this.

My brain short-circuited. I felt like sparks were going off in my head as all the little neurons and whatever went crazy, while all the blood in my body was sinking down to my groin. Alex's mouth was so damn warm as he bobbed back and forth, swallowing more and more of my cock. He flicked his tongue over the head every time he pulled away. Without realizing it, I'd somehow fallen towards him and was only keeping myself upright by the first grasp I had of his hair, which was smooth and grabbable and smelt faintly of apples.

"I hope you bloody meant it," he said as he pulled away, falling backwards onto the bed and taking me with him, "otherwise this probably counts as sexual assault."

"Feel free to assault me any time," I said in return, using my weight to pin him to the bed and seeking out his mouth to take possession of it with a kiss.

He tasted good. He tasted so, so good, and I could feel his cock swelling and growing beneath me—could appreciate the way he was hitching his hips so that we were rubbing against each other, so that we were frotting like desperate teens who might not know exactly what they wanted but knew what felt good.

It was all a bit blurred from there. Alex opening up underneath me, the slop of the lube against my fingers, covering the condom. The moment I pushed in, and he said "God, there," his voice gravelly with desire. Then he rolled over so he was on top, literally fucking himself on my cock as I slid fingers, still slicked with lube, up and down his shaft. Powerful thighs meant that he was totally relentless. He took me in to the hilt before withdrawing and then doing it again, harder, faster. I could hear his breathing become rougher, feel his movements becoming less smooth, see the drops of sweat slipping down his torso.

I came first, my fingers involuntarily tightening on his cock. But he wasn't far behind me, his own release covering us both in salty white cum. He collapsed on top of me, sweaty brow against my shoulder, taking groaning breaths which were so damn sexy that if I hadn't been so truly fucked already, I would be been hard and horny in seconds.

"This was not—" he panted at last, "—what I had in mind when I asked you to photograph me."

"Really?" I couldn't stop a silly grin plastering itself across my face. "I haven't been thinking of anything else for months."

He lifted his head, and to my amusement he was blushing like a virgin. "I didn't say I hadn't fantasized about it. I just reckoned that having you take my picture was the closest I was likely to get to …" His blush increased, and he trailed off.

"Were you propositioning me?" I demanded, wondering if I'd heard right.

"No-oo, not exactly," he countered. "I didn't think you'd be interested. But I just thought that … having pictures of me in your bed … might be the next best thing." He dashed a hand across his face, ostensibly to push his sweaty hair out of his eyes, but I could see he was trying to hide his embarrassment.

"We could take them later," I said. "It wouldn't exactly be a hardship—unless I couldn't keep my hands off you, which is quite likely. Or I could even take photos of you now." I looked down at his sex sated body, still feeling my heart race just at the sight of him. "I'm sure they'd sell within seconds. Only I don't think I'd want to share them ..."

WILLING AND ABEL

Abner Ray

It was inconceivable at the time to consider how the events of a single day might have a lasting impact on a person's entire life. It seemed like a dramatic device that I'd read about in novels and watched on TV. I guess I was too cynical even at that young age to believe it could happen to me. But it did. There was one twenty-four-hour period that took place that would become the catalyst for all my romantic and sexual activities for the rest of my life.

This summer of 1982 would mark my memory as a period of many firsts and many awakenings. I'd just arrived in Los Angeles in the early hours following a bumpy red-eye flight from Columbus, Ohio. I'd just graduated from college and had eagerly accepted a very gracious invitation from my somewhat distant uncle Stewart to spend the summer in his guest bungalow, which was separated by a sparkling kidney-shaped pool from his rather modest (by Beverly Hills standards, anyway) Spanish villa. As someone who went to college only a few miles from his hometown, this seemed the opportunity of a lifetime. My family was conservative without much money, and I'd wandered rather aimlessly through the previous four years being the honor student and dutiful son, attending church, working odd jobs to help put myself through school and, of course, dating girls in whom I wasn't the least bit interested.

I was very innocent in many ways when I arrived in this City of Angels.

I hadn't set my travel alarm clock that first morning, so I slept until nearly noon, which was incredibly late considering I was still operating on eastern time. I was awakened by what sounded like someone splashing in the pool. When I'd arrived the previous night, Stewart had said he was leaving town before sunrise and I'd have the place to myself, so I leaped out of bed, pulled on the pale blue corduroy Ocean Pacific shorts I'd purchased just before the trip, and went outside to see who was there. As I hit the warm California sunshine I'd heard so much about, I could smell the fragrant night-blooming jasmine that surrounded my doorway. Then I saw his head pop up from the pool water. When he saw me, he lifted his hand and waved vigorously. From where I was standing he appeared to be swimming nude.

When he emerged from the aquamarine pool, I could see that he wasn't naked after all. He was wearing white Calvin Klein underwear (still a novelty at that time) that were made completely sheer by their wetness. I tried to divert my eyes and look up into his, but instead found myself almost hypnotized by the clinging briefs as I caught a glimpse of the bushy dark hair surrounding the thick pink bulge pushing against the fabric.

As a natural blond, I have to confess that since the onset of puberty I've been fascinated by dark pubic hair curling against light brown skin. There's just something almost intoxicating about the contrast of the colors and textures, and to this day the sight arouses me more than any little blue pill. I can trace it back to the first man I saw naked (my very hairy P.E. coach) in a shower room at my high school. Throughout my teenage years I'd feared this would be my downfall, that I'd be caught staring at naked brunet guys in the locker room. But somehow I managed to hide all those teenaged erections by kneeling down to tie my shoes and thinking of Mrs. Lambert, my elderly French instructor.

"Hi, I'm Abel," he said, extending his hand, causing me to look up into his eyes. "Mr. Swenson lets me swim in the pool when no one's here."

"I'm Jack," I replied, smiling and shaking his hand. His grip was firm and, as cliché as it sounds now, there was a charge between us the moment we touched. His hand was smooth and the skin had begun to wrinkle from his time in the pool. I noticed that droplets of water clung to the light fuzz on his lower arm. He toweled his hair dry and then shook it from side to side before standing up straight.

"You're Mr. Swenson's nephew," he offered, looking into my eyes. "He told me you were coming *later* in the week. I hope I didn't wake you." His tone sounded sincere, and I also detected an accent, which I presumed was Mexican.

"You didn't," I lied. "I've been up for a couple hours."

His lips pursed, then the corners of his mouth curved downward and his eyes blinked quickly. It was obvious he didn't believe me.

"Are you a friend of my uncle's?" I asked.

"I do some work around the house," he answered. "I repair things that need fixing. I'm very handy, as the expression goes." *A handsome handyman,* I thought. It seemed like something out of a corny soft-core movie. "I made coffee in the main house," he said. "I'll get you some. You wait here."

As he turned and walked away from me, the white, transparent underwear clung to him and I could clearly see the dark crack of his ass. *Wow, this guy could get me in trouble,* I thought.

From the kitchen I could hear that he'd turned on the radio; Men at Work's "Who Can It Be Now?" was playing. He promptly returned with a tray with two cups of coffee and handed me one. We sat next to one another on the lounge chairs near to the pool and made polite conversation.

Abel was definitely a piece of work, I'd learn that day. I could tell immediately by his sly grin and the twinkle in his eyes that he was used to getting his way, probably because he was so breathtaking. I was immediately struck by his eyes, which were almost feline and the palest shade of green I can remember seeing. His lips were full and red, as if he'd just bitten them to make their color more vivid. They were apparently also very dry, as his tongue flicked out of his mouth on occasion to moisten them. Then, as ridiculous as it sounds, the wind began to rustle the palm fronds and a beam of sunlight hit the back of his head, creating a glow around his head that was practically a halo. Perhaps his mother should have named him Angel instead of Abel.

We spent the afternoon chatting and swimming and lunching on sandwiches he made. By mid-evening, the sun began to set.

The margaritas were his idea. And as I took the glass from him, some of the liquid spilled over the side and landed on his bare foot. His free hand quickly and tightly grabbed my forearm to steady it. "I don't want you to spill any more of your first margarita," he said, as the corner of his lips curled mischievously.

"It looks both delicious and refreshing," I offered. *God, what a lame thing to say. Keep it together.*

Obviously aware that I was nervous, he said, "Wait until you taste it." Then, looking straight into my eyes, his mouth opened into the sly smile the Cheshire cat would have admired. "I hope it's not too strong."

It felt like a dare. I took a mouthful and swallowed. The salt from the rim of the glass caught in my throat and I coughed.

"Easy there, tiger," he cautioned. "Don't choke on it."

We both laughed.

"I'm so sweaty and there was so much chlorine in the pool. Do you mind if I take a shower in your room, Jack?"

Hoo, boy. He was playing with me now. Testing me. I decided to man up. "Not at all," I replied. "The door's unlocked."

He turned and walked away while I sat down on the lounge chair, wondering if I had the courage to take the bait. I'd been attracted to other guys for as long as I could remember, yet I had never acted on my sexual impulses.

As I opened the door to my bungalow, I noticed the shower wasn't running. Walking further into the room, I could see Abel stretched out on my bed, face down. Naked.

As he lay on his stomach, his light brown skin provided a deep contrast against the pale white sheets of my bed. His arms were folded beneath his head with his face turned to the right, facing the soft candlelight. The glow brought out the warm highlights in his dark brown mane of wet curls.

I noticed there was a tiny triangle of soft dark hair at the very base of his back pointing downward and continuing through the crack of his firm, shapely buttocks. His thighs were spread just enough that the underside of his scrotum was visible. His balls also had a smattering of dark fuzz on them. I wanted to put them in my mouth but fought the urge. What was I thinking? It had to be the margaritas. I tried to think of something to say. I didn't want him to know I was staring at his ass.

"I'm glad to see you've made yourself comfortable," I managed. I felt like I might hyperventilate at any moment.

"I'm so sleepy, Jack," he murmured. "But I think I've had

too much to drink—I don't think I can drive back to Hollywood."

With this he rolled over, and I could see that his penis was semi-erect. It had thickened up immensely from the outline I'd seen earlier through his soaked underwear. It was magnificent. Truth be known, I'd only seen one other erect penis besides my own, and that was when an obnoxious classmate popped a boner in the shower after gym and decided to make sure everyone saw it, even though he was ridiculed with the nickname "Pencil Dick" for months afterwards.

But Abel's was magnificent, the stuff of dreams—literally. It was so different from my own. Even at half-mast, the girth of it was more than I've seen in any penis since, and it was the color of the creamy coffee he'd served me earlier in the day. Abel's foreskin was stretched tight, allowing the purple mushroom-shaped head to be fully exposed. It was the cock I'd think about in the future whenever jerking off alone. I wanted to pounce on his body and run my hands all over him. I wanted to hold that spectacular cock and put my tongue against those round, furry balls.

But now that this moment had actually arrived, I was terrified.

He saw that I was staring. I tried to look away, but, honestly, I was hypnotized by the masterpiece I saw before me.

"I'm sorry if I've made you uncomfortable," Abel said. He rolled the r's in *sorry* and it sounded like a kitten purring. "I come from a very open-minded family. I love to be naked, but I apologize that I'm excited." His left hand gestured toward that beautiful erect cock, but he didn't look down at it. He continued to stare into my eyes, which eagerly met his.

"It's not a problem," I lied. "I've seen them before." But it was a problem. My cock was quickly becoming rock hard as well. I hoped my T-shirt hung low enough to obscure it. I saw him glance down, undoubtedly wondering if he was having an effect on me.

He knew exactly what he was doing.

"Jack, I want to ask you something, a favor," he uttered in almost a whisper.

Uh-oh, I thought. *This is going to be the moment of truth.* I summoned all the courage I could and responded, "Go ahead."

"My neck and back and shoulders are absolutely in knots," he shared, as he rotated his shoulders and made a face that seemed winced in pain. "I'd be incredibly grateful if you'd give me a quick massage."

I'm sure my mouth dropped open when I heard those words. This seemed like the gateway to paradise. Not only would I get to touch that incredible body, but I'd be doing it at his request. I couldn't speak, and there was a long silence until the candlewick crackled.

"OK," I replied with a nod.

"Ah, you're an angel," he said as he rolled over onto his stomach. "It doesn't have to be too aggressive. Have you given a massage before?"

"I used to rub my mother's shoulders at night. She said it helped her relax."

"Well, this might feel different," he suggested. "Come over here next to me on the bed."

I walked over and sat down. Thanks to my new friend Jose Cuervo, I was suddenly feeling confident, so I scooted over against him. I could feel the heat from his body, even through my clothing. I turned toward him and lifted one leg onto the bed so I could reach his shoulders. He folded his arms beneath his head with his face turned to the right, toward the nightstand. His eyes were closed and the glow from the candle reflected against his cheek. I put my hands on the back of his neck and began to shift my fingers in a circular motion before moving them to each side to apply pressure to his shoulders.

"You have big, strong hands," Abel told me. "Don't be afraid to use them."

I pushed harder against his shoulders. His back was smooth and pliable, and I could see that his skin was covered in light freckles from being in the sun today. I began to knead his flesh, going up and down from the top of his shoulders to the lower back, just above his tan line. He began to emit soft, almost inaudible moans. I was getting light-headed, and it wasn't just the alcohol. Something came over me and I leaned in and held my face close to his skin and inhaled. His scent was clean, like Irish Spring soap, but it was mixed with a hint of musk. He was intensely, effortlessly masculine, even while lying there in repose. My erection was about to burst through my shorts.

"Jack, I don't want to seem bossy since you're doing me a huge favor, but I'm afraid you're going to get cramps in your arms in that position," he said, turning his head slightly. "It will be a lot more comfortable for both of us if you straddle the back of my thighs."

It would be impolite to disagree.

I reached over my shoulder, grabbed the collar of my T-shirt, and pulled it off over my head because the sleeves were too confining. Although it was sticky from my sweat, I managed to peel it off in one jerk. I moved in closer to Abel and took in the view of his breathtaking ass before I straddled it as he suggested. He must have felt my stiff cock as I put my legs around him. His buttocks involuntarily clenched.

His buttocks! I looked down at them, mesmerized again by that sweet little patch of dark hair above his crack. As I began massaging his lower back, turning both hands in a circular motion in opposite directions, my thumbs brushed gently against the fuzz. I can barely convey the erotic sensation it created in me. Abel seemed to enjoy it as well. His body trembled. So much heat began to emanate from his skin that it felt like it was on fire. It was contagious. I gasped for breath.

"Are you OK back there?" he asked. He'd sensed what was happening to me. Or, more precisely, things were going according to his plan. I couldn't speak. Instead I took one finger and lightly traced the fuzz between his cheeks.

"That tickles," he uttered.

"I'm sorry," I replied. But I wasn't really sorry. I wanted to keep doing it. *Was this really happening?* I wondered. It seemed like a fever dream but I was invigorated and wanted to explore every inch, every nook of his body. My cock was throbbing.

"No, don't be," he insisted. "It feels good. Keep doing it."

His hips lifted a bit from the bed to encourage me. I spread his cheeks open a little with two fingers from one hand, and with the other I used two fingers to massage in deep between his crack. He began to emit the soft moans again.

"Are you sure you haven't done this before, Jack?"

I let out a deep breath and told him that I hadn't.

He immediately reached back with his left hand and pushed me back. Then he turned over. Before I could react, he sat up and grabbed my face with both his hands and leaned in and kissed me. His hands felt as warm as the rest of his body. I opened my lips and he pushed his tongue in. It made me tingle all over. He pulled back, looked at me, and smiled. The flickering candlelight made his eyes twinkle. I noticed that his cock had become trapped beneath the fabric of my shorts when he turned around. He backed up a few inches to free his huge boner and it bounced back and forth. I looked down and giggled.

"Do you like what you see, Jack?"

"I guess so," I replied.

"Let's cut the bullshit. We both knew this was in the cards when we met today."

He leaned in again to kiss me. There was a currency that passed between us when his tongue pushed my lips open. His hand moved to my face again and began to stroke my cheek. His tongue throbbed deeper into my mouth. I pushed back with my own, then raised my hand up to his head and ran my fingers through those tantalizing curls.

He withdrew his tongue and moved his mouth to my neck, which he began to kiss softly before pressing his lips firmly against my skin. Abel knew what he was doing, and this created an erotic sensation I'd never experienced. I didn't know my cock could get any harder but I could now feel pre-cum oozing out. I looked down and noticed that one of Abel's hands was on his cock. He'd pushed his foreskin down and was rubbing the slit, which was also leaking pre-cum.

"Get those fucking shorts off," he ordered. He reached over and jerked the zipper down. I was still straddling him so I stood up, unfastened them, pushed them down, and wiggled my feet out of them. He grabbed them with one hand and flung them off the bed. My cock was standing straight out at full attention. No one had ever seen my erection before and I wondered what he thought of it.

"I see you're a natural blond," he cracked. We both smiled. I was still standing, and he reached up and touched my pubic hair, ran his fingers through its fullness.

"I've never had sex with a blond man before," he revealed, looking up at me with a mischievous glean in his eyes.

"I've never had sex with a man before," I shared.

"Then this is going to be the greatest night of your life, my friend." He reached up, took my hand, and pulled me back down to the bed. I crossed my legs underneath me, partly from comfort, but mostly because I was embarrassed to be so exposed. Abel moved closer and wrapped both his legs over mine. The curly dark hair of his legs felt prickly against the finer, lighter hair of my own. The colors and textures of our bodies created a complete contrast against each other, even in the dim light. But this time his movement had smashed my own erect penis, lodging it beneath his scrotum. As if it had a mind of its own, the swollen head of my cock was jabbing against his hole. He reached down and freed it while gripping it softly.

"You have a nice dick, Jack," he said with characteristic directness. "But let's not get ahead of ourselves."

His hand stroked my shaft a few times. It felt unbelievably good, certainly much better than my own hand ever did. His fingers moved further down and lightly grazed my balls, and the feeling was absolute bliss. Then he pressed the index finger lower until it got dangerously close to an area I wasn't comfortable having him explore—at least not yet. There was no need to rush, he'd said. This was something I wanted to take nice and slow.

I took his hand, pulled it up from my crotch, and locked my fingers with his own. I leaned into kiss him but then everything seemed to change. Abel, suddenly full of energy, kissed me hard on the lips then began working his way slowly down to my chest. He kissed and licked my nipples, nibbling at them with careful teeth. The sensation drove me wild. I ran my fingers through the dark tangle of curls on his head and then massaged his shoulders while his tongue traced a line down the center of my smooth abdomen to my navel. Before I knew it, his tongue was teasing the swollen head of my cock. So much for going slow, I thought. I moaned loudly—and uncontrollably—as his thick lips took my cock head and my stiff meat slid deep into his mouth. He took it all in, then pulled back all the way to the rim of the head and sucked it all in again. It felt even better than I'd imagined. This was heaven and he was God. My body began to writhe and my legs flexed and pawed for traction as he gave me the greatest sucking I'd ever experience. Then he slipped my cock out of his mouth and started flicking at my balls with his tongue. Soon he'd managed to get both in his mouth. I looked down with awe at his swollen cheeks, marveling silently at his skill, then I closed my eyes and leaned back onto the pillow to enjoy more of this.

Then it stopped. I sat up to see what had happened and he looked at me with that devilish grin.

"Jack, now it's time to see how far you really want to go."

Abel pushed my face down to his crotch and I duplicated every trick I'd just learned from him. I licked at the tip of his cock and tasted the salty fluid that seeped from it. I tried to take all of it deep in my mouth but I was still too inexperienced, and choking would have humiliated me. Instead I went further down and began to kiss his balls and suck them, one at a time, into my mouth. He squirmed with sheer pleasure. I licked all around his balls before my tongue pressed deep into the fuzzy area of his inner thigh, against his scrotum, and traced a line till I found myself underneath his ball sac. The pressure of my hard tongue against this unexplored area made him wriggle and his breathing got heavier.

He began to say my name over and over, as if it were an incantation. I continued to work my way down, further and further. My tongue was stiff and on fire with desire for the taste of him. Then something came over me, as if giving me some kind of silent instruction, and I impulsively grabbed both of his legs and hoisted them over my shoulders. I buried my face into that spectacular ass

I'd lusted for just minutes ago, and I found nirvana. I licked all around his tight pinkness, pushing my tongue through the curls that surrounded it. I pushed my tongue in and his hand pushed down on the back of my head as he spread his thighs wide to give me better access. My eyes darted up and I saw that his other hand was stroking his cock slowly and methodically. I continued licking and then I pushed one finger inside his hole while I rimmed the outside. He reached down and pulled my hand away from his ass.

"Jack, my God!" he exclaimed. "Not with your finger."

I could take a hint. I reached down and groped my dick, which was still rock hard and pulsating. I spit onto the fingers of my other hand and rubbed the saliva all around his still-wet hole.

Then, in one quick move, I pushed my erection inside of him, gently with just the head at first. Moaning again, he reached down and helped spread his cheeks even further apart, and my cock slid in all the way with ease. I pushed in until my balls banged against his now-sweaty crack and he began to stroke his own meat faster and faster. His ass clenched my thick shaft and it felt like ecstasy. I don't know how long I fucked him, but it seemed like only a few seconds before he began to pant heavily.

"I'm going to cum!" he warned, reaching up to push against my chest.

I pulled out of him immediately as directed and saw that a thick, white fluid had been shot all over his abdomen. I closed my eyes and gave my own dick a few more strokes. My body began to tremble with an electricity I'd never before felt while jerking off. My load exploded from my cock and landed with a splat all over his. As I gasped for breath, I saw that he was smiling.

"That was fantastic," he told me.

"It was incredible," I said, laying on top of him and feeling the stickiness of our cum forming a bond between us. I closed my eyes and within seconds I was in a deep slumber.

The sunlight beamed through the window and I felt the warmth of it hit me in the face. I slowly opened my eyes, squinting. I could feel there was no one else in my bed. I looked over but Abel was gone, and apart from the dried white flakiness on my chest, there was no sign he'd even been there.

My uncle returned later that morning, but I could never summon the courage to ask him for information about his handyman—the one who'd become *my* handyman. I kept hoping that one day he'd just be there, in the pool or in the garage. Somewhere. But Abel didn't return the entire summer, and sometimes I wonder if I imagined him, this man who—in his own words—"repaired things that needed fixing."

Because he was exactly what I needed to activate a part of me I'd been hiding.

While I never encountered Abel again in the flesh, I still feel his presence and the changes he inspired in me every day.

JUMP-START
Gregory L. Norris

I.

You can't get away from Palm Springs, the Greater Los Angeles Area, or the West Coast fast enough, so you book a flight from LAX to Logan International Airport, hoping you won't melt before departure. It isn't really hot here, not at this time of the year, and the temperature's hovering somewhere close to the south of zero where you're headed, but you're burning up on the inside. You've been on fire for days, unable to catch your breath or sleep. You gulp down water and iced coffee by the gallon. Panic attacks, your highly paid doctor tells you. You dump the pills, attempt to wrangle the problem under control through Zen philosophy. And when that fails, you flee for icier climes.

You pack smartly. It's cold where you're going. Luckily, a shoot the previous winter took you to Aspen, so you already had a decent coat, gloves, and a ski hat in your closet. You ordered long-sleeve shirts from the Bean catalogue and paid for overnight shipping. If they didn't make it to your front door before you fled California, well, fuck it—you certainly could afford to pick up replacements when you hit New England. You're better than well off after twenty years of jerking your giant dick for the camera, fucking sometimes when the price was right or the mood struck you, mostly getting fucked by an endless parade of stunt cocks. So many men, so many dicks. Too many. Your career stretches all the way back to the late, lamented VHS tape, with the DVD sandwiched between it and streaming high-def video.

The panic sets in on this, the first week when there's no work booked, and your agent, Barry Waterford—yup, just like the crystal—has stopped returning your calls. Sex, even the worst of it, has always been a centering force for you. Without it, you've paced your bungalow in the Hollywood Hills, suffering the human version of a nuclear meltdown—without that regular maintenance, the system burns up, explodes, plummets through cracks in the earth, all the way to China.

You could escort, sure, like a lot of gay porn actors following the twilight of their careers. But you're not some fly-by-nighter, in it for a year or so, in it only for the money. You're Cory Cox (née Arthur Fallender), a name, face, and dick as revered and recognizable as Ridgeston's, Idol's, Atlas's, or Stryker's. The term "porn star" gets tossed about too easily, but you're it, the genuine article. Or at least you were.

No, no fly-by-night member of an exclusive club. Even so, you hop the red-eye flight, business class, hoping no one will recognize you at this late hour, now that your career is over, whether officially or unofficially—it doesn't matter which. You have to get away before all the pent-up energy still creating chemical reactions within your flesh ignites and consumes you.

You went online, searched real estate ads for rentals and sales. You found the chalet-style house in a remote town in Vermont whose name sounded like poetry—Willoughby. When you were in Aspen, you got happy again. Something about the roaring fire, the falling snow, reactivated parts of you that you assumed were dead. Only dormant—switches were thrown back to the "on" position, and you experienced a jump-start of sorts, a reprieve from the inevitable meltdown looming on the horizon.

You board business class. There are a few bodies scattered about—businessmen mostly, you assume by their dress. California cocksmen off to other coastlines, where they'll squeeze out big deals to fill corporate coffers. You turn away, wait for the cabin lights to dim, cuddle down beneath the blanket you're offered, and pass out, exhausted.

Aspen.

They were a couple of snowboarders. Young dudes, adrenaline junkies. One said his name was Jason. He was tall and lean, wore his dark hair in an athlete's cut, no facial scruff. The one called Bradley had a shaggy mop and a goatee that made your dick toughen.

You caught them staring while you sat in front of the big fireplace in the lodge, feeling good for the first time in forever. Great, in fact. You didn't exactly know why other than that you were out of southern California and the air was cooler, easier to breathe. Nobody at the ski lodge knew there was a gay porn flick being filmed upstairs on the third floor; all of the cast and crew were instructed to be discreet.

But you were Cory-fucking-Cox, and there was no way to disguise the fact that your face—and monster dick—had gotten plenty of notice around the planet. Naturally blond, blue-eyed, with your pouty lips and dimpled chin, your hypnotic image had graced untold numbers of video boxes, DVD cases, and magazine covers. The amount of seed squirted out of your nut sac over the years is nothing short of super-human. *Could fill a city reservoir,* you once joked in an interview following one of your gay video award wins. You're not a household name per se, but a lot of men around the globe recognize the face that launched a thousand strokes.

You feel the slither of their eyes over your flesh, tip a glance up to see two young demigods recently returned from the slopes ogling you from across the room. Athletic, straight, you assume, by outward appearances. Then you remember that sexual identity isn't as black and white as it was even a decade ago. Their generation has progressed past "bisexual" to whatever feels good at that moment. Jason—you'll later learn his name—moseys over, looking slightly nervous. You see the meaty weight at the front of his pants, a bona fide *bone* popped over you, and know what's about to happen.

"Hey," he says, leaning down close enough that you catch the intoxicating scent of his fresh male sweat. "You that dude who can suck his own dick when he's getting fucked?"

"Guilty," you confess.

"Room 213, if you're into it."

You glance at Jason, who chokes down what must be a hell of a dry fucking swallow. Tempted, you steal a look at his lump. A wet spot now caps his erection. Then you focus on the other one, the scruffster, the second hopeful star fucker.

"213?" you somehow manage, aware of how stiff you yourself have gotten over this offer of a sweaty three-way with a couple of hot strangers.

Jason flashes a smile, and suddenly he's sexier to you than all of the dick you've hummed on over the years—and you've enjoyed the best! You were one of the first to wiggle your tongue between the toes of gay-for-pay stud Girth Brooks and eat his furry hole with such skill that the dude busted while you were in mid-lick. You bottomed for that tender, tragic teddy bear, Arpad Miklos, and

149

some nights still dream about him, waking with tears in your eyes and phantom tingles in your fuck-hole.

But this prospect makes you feel like a virgin again, one who's about to pop his first load in something other than his own hand or the dirty gym sock he swiped from his best friend's laundry pile.

Jason struts away. He and his scruffster pal give you tips of their chins, a gesture that's part of the human male's most primitive language. An invitation to wrap your lips around a pair of hairy jock dicks, lick the sweat off what you assume are two decent sets of low-swinging balls, and honor them with an encounter they'll never forget.

Turns out, you won't forget it, either.

Getting from the comfortable chair set before the roaring fire in the lodge's great room up to 213 seems to take you hours, not minutes. The scruffster answers the door. Enough time has passed for Bradley to kick off his ski boots along with his socks. Your breaths come with difficulty at the sight of those big, bare boats. Men's feet have always been among your favorite body parts, as viewers who've followed your work over the years know. Depending upon the man, of course. This man may be among the finest you've ever encountered.

"Dude," he says real cool and opens the door wider, welcoming you to enter. "Bradley." He aims a thumb at his chest, presently showcased in a T-shirt tight enough to display the magnificent torso beneath. "You've met Jason."

Bradley holds top stud status for another second or so before he's forced to share bragging rights with his good buddy. Jason's barefoot, too. Their room is a mess, typical of horny young jock dudes likely on some sort of winter break from their equally messy frat house. Clothes and snowboards share space with unmade beds. An air of musk hangs over the place. Jason's dick appears, thrusting up from his unzipped jeans, a thick, long beaut sporting plenty of fur around its root. Two nuts as meaty as you assumed spill down below it, begging to be licked.

"You don't waste any time," you joke, reach out, and boldly pump the young demigod's dick.

Jason moans a deep and breathless, *"Fuck,"* and rises to the tops of his toes.

Bradley moves closer, sandwiching you between two warm, muscular bodies. He brushes his mouth across your ear, and all that facial scruff prickles your flesh, eliciting a gasp.

"Delivery Days," he growls.

You instantly know the meaning—one of your most famous roles, that of the experienced pizza parlor owner who hires horny blue-collar deliverymen by getting them to deliver their loads first in his private office after hours.

You experience the odd rush of emotion that comes from being recognized by your fans, caress Jason's pulsing thickness, and tip a look at the nearest window. It's snowing again, you see. Your dick complains at its confinement inside your jeans. When was the last time you were so hard without needing the services of a fluffer? You love sex; love sucking and licking and getting fucked. But this doesn't feel like work. Not one bit.

"You're the fucking hottest," Jason huffs. And then he lists some of your professional highlight reel's greatest hits, including that bit you sometimes do when you suck on your own cock and your pre- dilection for worshipping another dude's feet.

You feign modesty, promise to tongue the buttery stink from between his sexy toes just like you did to Girth, and reach behind you, locating the bulge in Bradley's pants.

Then you're on the bed in an awkward tangle of limbs. Bradley's mouth sucks hard on Jason's dick. You steal a few laps off Jason's nuts, which are fragrant from the manly sweat he worked up riding the slopes, before you move on to Bradley's goods. He's uncircumcised, with a fleshy snout that hugs his dick's head like a collar even fully stiff.

"Sweet," you whisper, and then hum.

You love uncut cock. You've slurped on plenty of hooded dick though never enough. While gobbling down Bradley's and playing with his balls, you grow aware of your pulse. Your heart beats a frantic tattoo over the joy discovered in Room 213. You assume the organ's been there all along pumping blood through your circulatory system; why, just this morning, you bottomed for Riley Rocket, one of the industry's sexiest up-and-cummers. You went down on him in the luxury suite one floor up, and he fucked you without mercy on the faux-bearskin rug before cameramen and crew, business as usual. Still, it dawns on you that, until you're sucking on a stranger's balls, you've become an automaton. You've stopped feeling and have been only going through the motions. Your body isn't ruled by a beating heart but by the organ between your legs.

You feel something now as you sniff and lick at Bradley's luxurious folds of cock-sock and look up, seeing his goatee wrapped around his buddy Jason's dick. This is *fun*. It makes you feel like a fresh, horny young male at the start of his career, not sliding toward the end of it on the congealing puddles of semen left over from countless former money shots.

Aspen.

You thought about going back there, but Colorado's too close to Cali. Anyhow, Jason and Bradley are long returned to wherever they live. Vermont's better. A blank canvas. Besides, if you don't dig in your heels in New England, the next stop is a plunge into the Atlantic.

The plane rumbles through the dark night sky, headed toward the frigid East Coast. Memories of your encounter in Aspen linger after you stir awake. You swear you can taste the bitter magic of Bradley's foreskin and smell the sweat from his nuts. You even feel one of them tugging on your dick, mesmerized by their good fortune from encountering true celebrity Johnson at the ski lodge. Pulling on it, pumping your thickness in playful, awkward fumbles. You tell them it's OK—they can suck on it, too, after you put on the big, freaky sideshow and autofellate yourself. You're as clean as they come, thanks to routine STD tests. Go ahead, hum on that big old bad boy …

You rouse fully, aware that either Jason or Bradley has jumped out of your dream and into real time. Specifically, into the previously unoccupied seat next to yours. In the dim light, you make out a two-hundred-dollar haircut over a tie that probably cost as much and smell the expensive cologne slapped onto the neck of one of the merciless businessmen riding the air at forty thousand feet with you. He's somehow unzipped your pants beneath the blanket and helped himself to *your* business.

The last good traces of your dream down memory lane evaporate. The irony strikes you—this, here and now, is a scene right out of some porn flick you could have acted in. Only it's really happening. There aren't any cameras.

"Cory Cox," the man grumbles, as though that alone gives him license to sample the merchandise.

He squeezes your bone with another upward stroke beneath the blanket, flashes you a smug smirk. You ought to charge, you think. Charge the fucker for the privilege of tugging on your legendary stick. Maybe the nervous heat rising inside you at the thought of retiring from the only business you've ever known will dissipate.

Instead, you push the fucker's pedicured hand away, zip up, and move to another seat.

II.

You land and pick up your rental. It's nothing fancy, though the four-door's blue, your favorite color. With the bottle of water you paid for at an airport gift shop and the satellite radio tuned to eighties easy listening, you head north on Interstate 93, hop onto I-89 in Concord, New Hampshire, and cross over into Vermont right as the gray January sky reminds you the days are much shorter now. They sure as fuck are colder here! According to the temperature displayed in digital numbers on the dashboard, it's in the single digits outside, enough to count on the fingers of one hand.

You run the heat, thankful you dressed appropriately before boarding in California, and drive. The chalet in poetic-sounding Willoughby still seems a million light years away, though the GPS tells you that you're almost there. Snow falls in dusty flakes swept across the road by the wind.

Your stomach rumbles, reminding you that you haven't eaten anything in hours. The lack of sleep and a hint of jet lag are also catching up. The cold lays heavy and oppressive. The temperature drops another two fingers. The chalet has a woodstove, you know. If you're not too exhausted, you'll build a fire, maybe jerk your dick and revel to those great memories born of your time in Aspen. A smile twists on your mouth. Feels alien, that gesture. Maybe, you muse, it's time to wear a new face for whatever new hat Fate has lined up for you now that offers to whip it out professionally have stopped coming in.

In Willoughby, you spot a gas station—a good sign, considering you're down to half a tank—and pull in to fill up. Next door is a diner. Also good, because your stomach needs refueling. A wrecker idles, just off to the side of the pumps, McDermott Towing written across the door. Inside the building, you spy a tall dude standing at the register with his back to the door. Seeing him unleashes a chill through your body, one having nothing to do with the weather. Your teeth chatter as you swipe your bankcard and wait for the dials to reset. You suck down a breath and insert the nozzle into your gas tank and pump the good stuff in, trying not to compare the activity to all the fucking taking place far away in California without you. The frigid gust of wind that engulfs you helps. You've never been this cold. It's exhilarating.

You fill the tank, return the nozzle, take your printed receipt. As you hurry back to the driver's door, the tall man exits the gas station. Your eyes connect for a second or so, and in that bottled gaze you forget how many hot men you've slept with over the years. Slates and lists get wiped clean. You'd trade twenty years of constant busting for one chance to have him. Long, lean face covered in the scruff of what you imagine is a few days' worth of prickle, his body breathtaking even in winter coat, old blue jeans, older boots, he is, you agree, the handsomest man who ever lived.

"'Sup?" he growls, and tips you his chin along with a trace of a smile. "Nice fucking weather."

"The nicest," you answer.

"Yup," he says, and heads toward that big truck idling at the side of the pumps. "Keeps me busy."

He gets in and backs out. As he swings past, you see his face closer up, spiral into the gravitational pull of his vibrant blue eyes, and fall in love with his mouth, those lips wreathed in manly scruff, the lower of the two plumper than its twin on top.

The dude grins at you as he pulls away, leaving you hot all over again in spite of the deep freeze. Instead of burning up, though, this feels different. Like you're coming alive, back from the dead. A phoenix rising up from the ashes.

You order a burger at the little chow shack. Not one of those taste-less vegan soy things with avocado, but a giant made of grass-fed beef, with real cheese and bacon on it. Fries, too. You wash it all down with a chocolate milkshake and realize it's the first meal you've enjoyed in a long time. You actually *taste* the food, and love every bite.

The chalet sits surrounded by trees, on the other side of a treacherous bend that winds around a mountain. You park your rental in the driveway, lug your bags in, and crank the heat. After a quick tour, you build a fire in the woodstove and absorb your new surroundings. The restless mountain wind blows around the house, but you feel safe in Willoughby. After all, he is out there, providing roadside assistance to any and all who get into trouble.

You snuggle onto the sofa before the woodstove, unzip your pants, pull out your dick, and do that famous trick, reliving the sound of his voice while pretending the fat cock in your face is his. And after you cum, you again catch yourself smiling.

You wake and go through the motions in a strange, new place: brew coffee and enjoy it in a deep cup you find in a cabinet, then shower and dress. There are plenty of staples in the kitchen pro-vided for renters, but nothing fresh or extravagant, which means another trip into town.

Only when you wander outside into the sub-zero temperature that greets you on this early Saturday morning do you discover your rental is dead, a frozen block of metal. You figure it's the bat-tery—cold weather gobbles them up with the same hunger you slurped on your own dick.

Mouthing a breathy, *"Fuck,"* you tromp back into the house.

No biggy, you think. You have insurance on the rental, plus all those A's on your sports car parked in the garage back at your house in California. You think of your options, decide on one you didn't count on until yesterday, and find the number after a quick search on your phone. You dial.

A sleepy voice answers. "McDermott's."

Your entire body comes alive. "Yes, I need a jump-start," you say, rattling off your real name and your new temporary address.

"I can be there in fifteen," he says.

It feels like the longest quarter of an hour of your life. Then you hear the hammer of your heart playing in counterpoint to the grumble of the McDermott's Towing wrecker as it chugs around the mountain and up your driveway. You glance out the window. The cold has robbed the new day of its luster, but you swear the sun is shining directly on him when he gets out of the cab and struts toward the chalet's front door. Suddenly, breathing takes effort. You record the details of his body again. His face is even handsomer than you remember. Dark, neat hair under a base-ball cap and giant feet complete the snapshot. You steal a look at his package on his final approach and ignite all over again to thoughts of how he's probably worked most of the night, kept busy by the cold; how fragrant his nuts must be at this early morning hour.

You answer the door right as he readies to knock with one of his big, bare hands. The cold pours in, laced with the clean, masculine scent coming off his body—the dregs of deodorant mixed with sweat. He does a double take, grins.

"You," he says. "Thought I recognized your car."

"My car?" you challenge, aware of his eyes on you, absorbing every detail in like.

157

He's a man who services untold hundreds of cars—a dude who could have any hole he wants. He hovers, smile fixed upon his face. You've seen that look before plenty of times when fans engage you. You hope he's starstruck and that you're not hallucinating his interest.

"You look familiar," he growls.

"I get that a lot."

There's some more small talk. He tells you his name—Dave McDermott. Maybe the sexiest name you've ever heard, you think. You shake hands. His almost crush yours. Then you're both back outside. He hooks his jumper cables to your rental and asks you to turn the digital key in the car's high-tech ignition. The car rumbles to life.

"Let it sit and charge up," he says.

You suggest that you both wait inside. There, you offer him coffee. He says he'd love something else to heat him up. The air radiates with invisible static. Dave reaches for you and pulls you into a manly hug. You drink in his scent, revel in the rough scrape of his cheek against yours. A moment later, you're on your knees in front of him, fumbling with his zipper. You get it down, work on releasing his belt. The black boxer-briefs hugging his flesh are rich with his sweat.

You wonder if you're still asleep on the plane, dreaming up the entire scenario, being jacked by a businessman's unwanted hand. No, when you pull down his underwear and Dave's hairy root snaps up, so stiff that his dick has already turned plum-purple from excitement, you know this is real. The funky sweat on his balls testifies to long work hours and makes you salivate. You suckle them, feeling more alive than you can recall. Even more so than when you were in Aspen.

A few stiff sucks on Dave's cock, and then he pulls you up to your feet. He backs you toward the bedroom, grabbing at your ass. The rest of your clothes come off. He tosses you onto the bed, spreads your ass, and feasts on your hole. The prickle on his hairy face reawakens every cell in your body. Your physique regenerates from his wet licks. Concentric waves of heat reach your deepest level. Deeper than marrow. Far past soul.

He compliments you on the size of your dick. "Bet you can suck it," he says, washing warm breath over your most sensitive flesh.

You always travel with condoms—old habits die hard. Before rolling one over his length, you beg him to honor a specific request.

"My feet?" he chuckles, though not in an insulting way. "Fuck yeah, dude. Anything you want."

He sits on the bed and you kneel between the hairy tree trunks of his legs. His feet are huge, sexy. You suck on each toe with the same devotion you showed to his dick. Dave clearly likes the attention, judging from the groans.

When he can't stand it any longer, he pulls you onto the bed, mounts you doggy-style, the wetness of his tongue in your ear nearly as electrifying as when it was in your butt or the slap of those fat, hairy balls as they gong against the patch of skin between your asshole and sac. Dave's nuts are the only things stopping him from fucking you all the way up to your esophagus.

"I love what you did to my feet," he grunts.

"I'll do it any time you want, stud," you promise.

"Yeah, good, 'cause I'm a horny fucker, and I need it a lot."

"I've got more tricks up my sleeve."

You maneuver beneath him, assuming a variation on missionary, suck your own cock between your lips, and put on a show, all with his dick still inside you.

"How long you planning to stick around Willoughby?" he chuckles, smiles.

And it becomes clear to you, just like that. A new life, mapped out to perfection. Fresh sweat pours out of your skin, washing away your worries. You're high on the heady male stink of Dave McDermott. Perhaps the best and biggest orgasm of your life builds toward release.

"Yes," you moan around your dick, and nearly choke on the deluge of whitewash you bust over your own tongue.

Dave leans down and kisses you hard on the lips and shaft as the cock buried balls-deep in your asshole, your *soul,* erupts in perfect synchronicity.

Outside, his big rig is still attached to your rental, pumping voltage, life, from one battery to the other. Inside, Dave is lodged in you, still hard, bringing you back from the abyss. He kisses your damp cheek.

"Tell me," you urge. "Which one of my movies is your favorite?"

"Movies?" he repeats in a playful voice.

"You said I looked familiar. You've seen my work?"

Dave shrugs, gazes into your eyes. His are blue, so blue, your favorite color. "Don't know what you're talking about," he says. "I saw you last night at the gas station and thought you were the hottest fucker I've ever seen. And all I've thought about since then is how much I want to fuck you."

Which he does again. And, you hope, he will do repeatedly in the days of your new life ahead.

POOL BOY
Brett Lockhard

There was nothing pretty about the dirt mountain that jutted from the desert floor, looming over the manicured lawns and impeccable midcentury estates. Reclining at the edge of the pool, Noah Mills let his feet sink in the water and pondered the Martian quality of this protuberance in the flat spread of desert, in the generally steady slope of the earth. What continued to draw him back to Palm Springs was the unexpected that sprang from the sunbleached gleam.

When his parents bought the house over sixty years ago, the dusty basin was just being discovered as a hideaway for Hollywood royals. As a child, Noah's weekends were confined to the pool enclosure of their Desert Modern retreat. With the passing of his parents, Noah made the town his own. Despite his history here, he still found a promise of sexy intrigue lurking in the dry heat.

By the pool, waves of oily light rippled across the rock garden. At 110 degrees, it was hard to think, move, or do anything at all. They had all been reduced to lizards, Noah felt, everyone in this town, crawling into the sun, finding a spot on rocky ground to bask in the oppressive heat. He thought of himself as reptilian—stripped to his basest instincts, incapable of nothing more.

L.A. was easy for him already. A movie producer with notable releases, he appeared like a montage of beach-house parties and terrace lunches. In Palm Springs, his formidable combination of clout, success, and enduring good looks translated to a series of easy pleasures. Young actors and dilettantes showed up at his door daily. Now thirty-eight, he felt pangs of the specific ennui endemic to those who had it all.

Now dry after a dip in the pool, Noah felt the day's first drops of sweat descend along the vein of his bulging bicep. He thought about last night's conquest, the newly appointed curator at the LACMA whose blond hair and bright skin still lay on Noah's pillow. He felt his thick cock swell in his shorts and knew he hadn't finished with the specimen inside. *What was his name again?*— *Jake,* he thought, nearly fully confident.

Approaching from behind, Noah took in the sharp lines of this man's torso, the slope of his ass, the cords of his thighs and calves—tight even as he slept. Growing fully hard, he hovered over the static form before sliding his tongue along the seam of the balls, exposed between parted legs, and into the warm, tight hole he had abused the night before.

Tracing a delicate circle around the rim, Noah made careful work of feeding the desire in Jake's ass. He retreated, blowing gently on the twitching pucker. With a slight tilt of Jake's hips, Noah's tongue sank deeper. A long baritone groan drowned in the pillow. Elbowing the legs apart, Noah spread him wider to accommodate the now-vigorous tonguing. A full inch deep, Noah reached for a fistful of blond hair and pulled his head off the pillow.

The sheets were covered with Noah's pre-cum. His tongue reached for the slick in order to smear it on Jake's lips. "I want you to …" He was interrupted by Noah's fingers in back of his throat. "You want me to fuck you?" he asked, turning him on his side to evaluate the masterpiece of his chest, the small pink nipples still raw from having been brutalized the night before. He slid three fingers into Jake's throat and forced another three deep into his ass. There were muffled pleas accompanied by an urgency in Jake's squinting eyes that Noah accepted as license for violation.

Holding Jake's head against the pillow, Noah guided his monster cock through his hole. As the inches slid in, he wrapped his strong arms around the man he was determined to ravage. He waited for a sigh. The spasm of tense muscle released, and Noah's entire thick length vanished.

Turning Jake's head, he trapped his gaze, spitting a huge wad into his mouth, open with anticipation. "Fuck, I love you inside me." He felt heavy balls with every thrust. Noah held him close. He made him feel protected even as he was abused. The thrill was almost too much to bear. He reached for his cock, a solid seven inches of throbbing meat, but Noah grabbed his wrist. "You don't get to cum yet."

"I won't cum. I just want to stroke myself".

"Well, you don't get to." Suffering was enough.

"Please, please, sir." The begging went on, more and more plaintive—until it was pure and urgent need. As Noah rammed him harder, faster, pummeling him now, he asked for more. He took pleasure in knowing it was no longer about touching himself; this was a man who could not possibly get enough.

"Pleeeaase," he said, gasping, desperate to catch his breath, the intensity of the fuck knocking the wind out of him.

In a moment of generosity, Noah lifted him to his knees and reached around, using pre-cum to lube Jake's cock, taking his time. He teased under the tip, slowly pulling out of his ass. With just an inch inside, Noah held still, ratcheting up the agony of this wait.

"Give it to me," Jake said, his abused hole hungry for more. "Fill me up, sir. I want to feel you let loose inside me."

"I don't know if you deserve it," said Noah, holding steady.

Outside a splash of water interrupted Jake's imploring moan. "What was that?" he asked, shocked to be aware of anything outside this room.

"Nothing. It's the pool guy."

Through the sliding doors, Jake saw a skimmer gliding across the surface of the pool.

"It's just an old man," Noah said. "He's been with us since I was a kid. Straight guy. Trust me, he doesn't care what's going on in here."

Relieved, Jake pressed his hips backward. Noah lost his cock deep inside. A seismic orgasm built up in both men, but Noah wanted to see Jake spew before relieving himself. The pounding was relentless, Noah's large cock slamming, hips chugging against the firm rounds of Jake's ass. Their fuck now reached a feverish pitch. Eyes squinting, he rumbled a protracted, euphoric groan. Four giant wads of cum landed in the soft fur of his belly as his body seized in an orgasmic spasm.

Noah buckled, allowing himself release. Jake's body writhing beneath him, ass tightening around the thick cock, he shot a gigantic load. It came in five distinct blasts, coating Jake's insides. Emerging from this animal rite, Noah's face softened.

The sound of the pool house door closing reminded Noah that they were not alone. He thought about Leo, the man who had taken care of the pool since he was a child. He was strong. A soft-spoken straight dude, arms like Tom of Finland, Leo was once what Noah had considered the ideal physical form—natural tan, furry chest, and forearms that told of years of rigor.

164

On summer break, Noah often found himself alone in his bedroom, watching Leo's every move. He remembered the cut of his calves, the Achilles tendon that made way to bare feet on the hot stone surrounding the pool. Noah pictured his ankles, the calloused hands, the accidental crevice of his obliques. His waistband sat just below his soft pubes. He remembered Leo's smell, the intoxicating mix of chlorine and sweat. Hoping to hide his growing erection, he thought about a slow, gravely voice and an intensity in his eyes—the disparity in their color contributed to his mystery.

Nothing ever happened between them, despite Noah's subtle provocations and endless daydreams. Before he had ever been with a man, Noah masturbated to the thought of his lips on Leo's salty skin, of the feral stench that endured in his fantasies, unrivaled to this day. *Was it because he was straight?* Noah thought. *Or was it something else?*

Perhaps it could never truly be identified, that quality in Leo that made Noah's cock come to life. Having just unloaded, after years of satisfying his cinema-worthy lusts, the mere recollection of Leo's smell made Noah squirm with desire.

Opening his eyes, Jake saw that Noah was somewhere else and knew that his time here was over. "I think I should hit the road."

Surprised to discover he was not alone, Noah snapped into focus. Always the gentleman, he said, "Don't feel you have to run off."

"It's time. I have a brunch thing," he responded, familiar with the game. "But thank you!"

"Pleasure was mine," Noah said as he watched the blond stud casually slip on his briefs before the rest of his clothes, his deliberately molded body a silhouette in the harsh light streaming in. He was perfect, and was about to disappear into the caverns of Noah's memory, where all these things were housed but rarely revisited.

Jake turned to Noah, lying on the bed, his cock half hard, heavy against his abdomen. Content in the post-fuck prolactin calm, his abused ass still hummed as he drove off with nowhere in particular to be.

The cold filtered air ran over Noah's naked body. He returned to thoughts of Leo. In his imagination he saw the hard lines of his arms and felt the three days of brown stubble on his jaw. He succumbed to his mystifying eyes—one the deepest chestnut brown, the other aqua. He reached for his cock and felt the head slick with pre-cum. Fully hard, he began stroking himself calmly, not necessarily trying to get off, teasing life out of an old fixation that should have gone stale by now.

Noah untied Leo's trunks, tugging on the zipper, trying to free his bulge. He imagined the smooth skin of his hard cock, the taste of his pre-cum—moving slowly around the tip, stopping to lick the length from slit to balls. The fantasy continued until he had tasted every part of him, slowly, then devouring—choking, gagging, begging.

He noticed the pace of his stroke accelerating. He looked up from Leo's hole and understood in his bi-colored eyes how badly the pool hand wanted to be fucked, right there on the lounge chair, under the brutal Palm Springs sun.

Noah tore into Leo, inebriated with the idea that he could be giving something back to this man, twenty years his senior, who had given him such lustful fodder over the years. If the physical pleasure of these solitary sessions could have been quantified and repayment attempted, it would have taken hundreds of marathon fucks to even begin. In the end there was nothing to reciprocate; the affair was merely a fantasy. It was both the most satisfying sexual relationship of his life and the source of endless agony—the bittersweet thrill of impossible love.

He held Leo by the bulbs of his calves, pressing the chalky soles of his feet to his lips as he pummeled him. Leo's ass was needy, his moans reverberant, their eye contact unbreakable. No words needed to be uttered. Noah understood the squint and slight nod of the head to mean Leo was ready. He reached for the giant cock with a spit-wet hand and stroked him toward completion. Leo bit his lip, made one last pleading gasp, and craned his head as he came.

It was the ultimate release. Cumming into the depths of Leo's hole, Noah bit his own lip in real life, tortured by the tension in his ample balls. Four shots landed in the dark curls of Noah's chest hair. He indulged in a helpless moan before melting into the prostrate relief of being fully spent.

Noah was unaware of the man outside churning out the last of his own leviathan load. Hardly the old man Noah had described, this guy was twenty-three years old—brownish hair, and an unmistakably Eastern European look that left him out of place among the preened faces in Palm Springs. He had a square jaw, among other trappings of classic masculine appeal: square pecs, arms made of iron. He also had big ears that could have looked oafish on someone else but somehow succeeded in making him even sexier.

Having taken advantage of the double feature Noah had unwittingly provided, the guy outside let his board shorts hang below his balls, the crack of his crescent ass exposed. He squeezed out the last drop of jizz and managed to shove the still-hard inconvenience back into his shorts seconds before Noah walked outside.

"Oh," Noah said, taking in the sight of this man he didn't know, his broad back tapering to a tight waist. The cords of his neck tensed as he looked up from the filter at the edge of the pool.

"Hi there," the stranger said as he stood up.

"I expected Leo."

"Sorry. Charlie here." He was standing now, making his way toward the owner of the house.

His handshake showed the unbridled power of a man in his prime, and Noah was reluctant to let it go. The confidence that coursed through Charlie was electric; he seemed raw and mysterious. Noah peered through his aviators, wondering if there was any sweetness in his eyes. In the glare he saw only his own reflection.

Careful not to seem creepy, Noah waxed professional: "Are you replacing Leo?"

"I thought he told you," Charlie said. "Sorry about that. The old man finally admitted that physical labor was not in the best interest of someone his age. He'll still run the business, but I'll be taking care of you from now on."

"I trust I'm in good hands. I'm off to buy some things for a party I'm having later. Nice to meet you, Charlie." Noah's smile was bright and effortless. It lingered in Charlie's mind.

But it was the thought of Noah's enormous cock, a thing he had just watched erupt phenomenally, that compelled him inside the house.

After the gate closed behind Noah, Charlie found himself drawn toward the sliding doors that opened to the bedroom. It was as if he had no agency in the trespass, no possible hope of denying himself this delicious impropriety. Stepping onto the marble floor, he noticed that the arctic temperature inside, which usually felt antiseptic in air-conditioned houses, was offset by the hormonal trace of recent sex.

He went immediately to the walk-in closet. He ran his hand along the button-down shirts pressed and hanging according to the color scale, a perfect symbol of cleanliness, order and refinement. Then he found what he had come in for: the hamper filled with dirty clothes. On top were the board shorts Noah had taken off before fucking Jake. Heart racing, Charlie brought them to his face and inhaled. The scent was chlorine and sweat; the thrill was being so close to this man who, minutes earlier, he had never met and to whom now he felt desperate to belong. In the mesh lining: a faint trace of white. He licked the lining, and— though just barely—he could taste him.

Now rock hard, Jake unzipped his shorts to relieve his cock, so big that it was nearly impossible to keep it confined in his shorts. He felt the slip of pre-cum around the head and caught it before it drooled to the floor. He could not resist smearing it over the spot already on the shorts and licking again, now imagining the wild indulgence of his cock pressed against Noah's.

Returning to the dirty clothes, he found a T-shirt and went hungrily for the pits. He reveled in the manly mix of sweat and deodorant. He reached deeper into the bin and pulled out a tube sock. Elated with how wrong it was, Charlie brought the sock to his face and took in the biting stench of a recent run. He wrapped it around his face like a gag and held the two ends tight behind his head.

Cock throbbing, it was a feat not to bring himself off on the floor of the closet. He was nearly in tears, desperate and yearning and overcome as he was with the scent of Noah's filth. But getting off now would mean the end. In the calm after cumming, he would clean himself up. He would cover any signs that he had been inside. His mind would return to real thoughts, to the errands the day still had in store, to the phone calls he had to return. Once he came, he would no longer be with Noah, and right now he was.

It was only the fear of being caught in the house that forced him out of the closet. He was so worked up he thought he might cum without even a stroke on his cock. Before leaving the house, however, he stopped at the bed and leaned over. Clenching the pillow in tight fists, Charlie filled his lungs with the smell; it was cool eucalyptus and sage tempered by the musk that sleep and sex had left behind. One breath was not enough for him. In reality he wanted nothing more than to be caught here; he was willing to suffer whatever punishment or embarrassment he would incur. But there was something else: the violation Noah might feel if he were to come and find the pool boy in his bed. It was a testament to Charlie's humility, to his heroic lack of hubris, that he leaned on this argument to pull himself from the pillow.

When he raised his head, he suddenly knew he was not alone. Terrified, he could not bring himself to look. Instead he stayed right where he was, resting on his forearms, staring blankly at the wall as he recognized what could only have been a footstep behind him.

Noah had been at the supermarket when he realized he needed more of the new pool boy—and he needed it immediately. He wanted so badly to be someone who shopped for his party unencumbered by biological demands, a person happy testing melons for ripeness. But right now being this person was not an option. What he needed was to see Charlie, to feel his body against his, to look into his eyes and discover whatever might be there to know. Never one to believe in love at all, never mind love at first sight, Noah felt silly acknowledging these thoughts, embarrassed by the cliché. But there he was, walking away from a cart filled with produce, unable to do anything before attempting to claim him.

When he opened the glass door to the bedroom, the vision of Charlie was electrifying. His desert-tan skin, the even coat of blondish hair that ran from under his shorts to his ankles, the shaggy waves of hair that hid his face. Noah approached slowly so as not to scare him, using all his willpower not to tackle him and take him from behind. He thought of them wrestling to the floor, tumbling with him in a frenzied passion, their gorgeous limbs in a sweaty knot.

170

Instead, he decided on brutal restraint and got on his knees. He crawled to within striking distance, then stopped. He did not move for some seconds, torturing Charlie with the tension that filled the hushed room.

The first contact he made was with his breath. Careful not to touch him, Noah put one arm on either side of Charlie's and let his lips hover over the innocent parts of him he wanted to devour—the nape of his neck, the small of his back. Only once he allowed himself to graze the hair on his forearm with his lips.

Finally indulging, he started to lick, tasting Charlie's skin, salty after a day spent sweating in the sun. He traced around his ear, along the slope of his neck, inebriated in the sweet, warm space between chin and shoulder. He found his way down the spine, then stopped again, ensuring that when he finally indulged Charlie's ass, it would be a satisfaction unmatched.

He left his shorts on and moved to the taut hamstrings—a soccer player's, Noah was sure. He moved gently from the back of the knee to the sculptural ridge of the calf. When he got to the ankle, Noah lifted the foot. When his tongue slid between the first two toes, Charlie let escape a helpless sigh, finally breaking the silence; it sounded like triumph and submission at once.

When the shorts came off, Noah spread wide the ass that he would soon take as his own, that he wanted to treat sweetly and violently. Not just right now, not just today, but over and over and over, into the future, until his hole belonged to him unequivocally. In truth he felt like it already was. He could not understand why or how, but he sensed he had known Charlie his entire life. There was no hope in Noah that he could ever tire of the thing before him.

He nosed into Charlie's ass and was overcome by the musk of a man who could only be his, who did not make sense being sniffed by anyone else. Noah felt he had arrived at a destination he had spent his entire life trying to find. He could not get enough. He resisted tonguing the ripe, firm ass because he wanted to revisit the scent of it just before the fuck that would be sweet and brutal in equal parts. He yanked the hips toward him, making room between him and the bed, then slid between Charlie's legs. What he found waiting for him was a cock that could have been a fantasy on its own. The fact that it belonged to this person, a source of limitless gifts, was hard to grasp.

Noah took his time with the head, but once the pool of pre-cum had been cleared, after a few smacks of the cock against his grateful tongue, he decided to show off a talent of his own. With both hands planted on Charlie's ass, Noah forced the monster cock deep into his throat, repressing even a trace of a gag reflex. Finally, breathing deeply, Noah was drunk in the smell of Charlie's pubes, a soft crop of brown hair, untrimmed.

Charlie took advantage of this expert mouth by fucking it hard. No matter how violently he slammed into Noah's throat, the only sounds he heard were grunts of pure pleasure. He was close to orgasm and wanted to make sure Noah could cum with him. He stopped thrusting and tried to pry his head from his crotch.

"I don't want to cum without you," Charlie said.

Noah made a noise that sounded like "OK" but continued to slobber, drooling, his mouth full of cock.

"Stop," Charlie pleaded. "I'm so fucking close. Please, I want you to fuck me." With the authority of someone desperate for cum, Noah grabbed both of Charlie's wrists with one hand. With the other he stroked himself vigorously to catch up. He slobbered up and down the enormous tool until his throat was flooded. As the jizz poured into him, he lost his own giant wad on the floor.

"I'll fuck you now," he said. "And we'll cum together again."

Charlie smiled as he was thrown onto his back. He felt his legs hoisted in the air. Feeling Noah's tongue glide into his hole, he real-ized he was not only rock hard, but dying for it. His entire body shook with renewed desire as Noah entered him, insinuating him-self inside, slowly at first, then waiting—but only for a second. As Charlie sighed, the ass opened generously; accommodating the scary-big dick was a challenge he was proud to accept.

Just as Noah's impressive length had descended fully into the depths, a needy grumble erupted in baritone waves. He knew it was time for the pummeling, for the forgetting of mercy, but before releasing his storm on this hungry ass, he wrapped his burly arms around Charlie's incredible body.

With his giant cock buried balls deep, Noah kissed him in a beautifully gentle way, and he meant it. When he opened his eyes, he saw Charlie's for the first time and smiled wildly.

Looking back at him were a pair of generous, soulful orbs: one brown, one the clearest blue-green, sparkling like pools of every-thing good in the world, of a lifetime of longing finally satisfied, like a life that was about to begin …

TOP CHEF BOTTOMS

Rob Rosen

It was my boyfriend's birthday present.

Wait, nix that. It was *to be* my boyfriend's birthday present.

No, no. Nix that as well—last time, promise. It was to be my *ex*-boyfriend's birthday present.

Yes, much better. Or worse. Depending on if you saw the glass as half empty or half full. Me, I was going with full. Full of ridiculously expensive vodka, that is, which he gratefully left behind. Fuck it. And him.

OK, bitter party, table for one.

Anyway, I'd canceled the party, uninvited all the guests—six in total, plus the two of us—returned the champagne, and got fucked by the DJ. Literally. See, he was going to charge me because I didn't cancel in time. My ass paid the penalty. Though with this particular DJ, the glass was certainly full and brimming over. And, yes, he spun me right round, baby.

In any case, with all the hubbub—the breakup, telling everyone about said breakup, drinking myself into oblivion, and the aforementioned DJ pounding—I might have forgotten one eensy, teensy, little something.

Though I did remember it ... just as the doorbell rang, the night of what was to be his birthday party, sans the birthday boy himself. *Oops.*

"Fuck," I cursed as I swung the door open.

He winced. "Um, yeah," he said, scratching his head beneath a white, fluffy hat. "This the Jefferson party?"

And then it was my turn to wince. "No party. No Jefferson anymore," I informed, a pit in my stomach blooming into a full-on lemon tree in mere seconds. "Hence the, uh, the *fuck.*"

He stared down at the tray in his hand and then back at the cart he was pulling. "Any hungry dogs on the premises then?" He smiled. It was a fetchingly toothy number. Meaning, somewhere there was an orthodontist with a rather large trophy case.

I shrugged and sighed, shoulders slumping all the while. "Just a finicky cat." I stared around him to the cart. "Any Puppy Chow on that thing?"

"For your cat?"

My shrug repeated. "Finicky *and* just a tad crazy," I explained. "Lord knows where she gets it from."

There was a pregnant pause. One of those nine-monthers. The kind where you want to push, but are afraid of the consequences. "Well, this is awkward," he finally uttered as he stood there, shifting from his left foot to his right and back again.

"Gross understatement," I replied, a flush of red working its way up my neck before splashing across both cheeks. "And I'll, uh, I'll pay you for everything, of course."

"You already paid," he told me. "Two weeks ago. When you confirmed all the arrangements. Including the sea bass I had shipped from Chile. Special order."

That red face of mine turned molten. Kilowea, in fact, had nothing on me. "Can't we just donate it all?"

175

His smile quivered, quaked, and promptly fainted dead away. "They don't take raw seafood at the shelter. Plus, I have a feeling the cook there doesn't have a clue how to prepare imported Chilean sea bass."

Suddenly, I hated my ex-boyfriend. That is to say, suddenly, I hated my ex-boyfriend even more than I hated him before I opened the door. "I can't possibly eat all this," I calmly explained.

His smile returned. It really was a nice smile. Nice everything, actually. He was young, slender, scruffy, and had eyes so startlingly blue you could just about take a dip in them. "I can cook it and you can freeze it. For later, I mean," he suggested.

I didn't have the heart to tell him that, post-breakup, my freezer was full of vodka and ice cream. "Or you can cook it and we can eat it together," I blurted out, staring at the cart again. "Or, um, most of it." My eyes landed on the tray he was carrying. "Or some of it, anyway."

Again he shifted from foot to foot. Poor guy. The tray looked awfully heavy, too. "I don't normally eat with the client."

I grinned. "And I don't normally eat enough food for eight people." I neglected to inform him that I could easily consume vodka or ice cream for that many people, though, if recent events proved anything. Fucking ex-boyfriend. "Think of our eating together as a tip then." His smile again quivered. "On, um, on top of the tip I was already going to give you. In cash." I held out my hand. "Justin," I quickly deflected. "And please have dinner with me. It's been a trying week." Again, gross understatement.

He sighed. "Well, I do love sea bass …" He shook my hand, balancing the tray as best he could as he did so. A spark of something akin to hope sizzled through my arm and promptly traveled down to my crotch. "Tom."

I grabbed the tray. He wheeled in the cart. The door shut behind us. *Click*. The sound made me jump, me and my heart and my prick.

He followed me to the kitchen, this stranger, a man I literally paid to be there. And, yes, it was that last thing that made my cock bob from within my jeans. Adding fuel to the fire was that fact that he was so friggin' cute. That and his chef's pants, which were super thin, the beguiling bulge clearly evident.

I gulped when I accidentally on purpose ran my index finger over his when we were setting everything up. He locked eyes with me in that moment, my gulp repeating as I found myself drowning in that stunning sea of blue of his. He smiled, and I dropped a bottle of mustard, Grey Poupon. So, yeah, I was apparently paying for nothing but the best.

"Sorry," I managed to squeak out.

"No worries," he said. "Let me get that."

I watched him bend over, his work pants sagging as he did so, a quarter inch of butt-crack revealed, a smattering of fuzzy black down sprouting forth, plus part of the elastic of some sort of underwear. I fought to not reach down and pull the material even lower. Still, it did give me a rather wicked idea, aided, of course, by the vodka I'd been drinking and the sugar from the vast array of ice cream I'd so recently consumed.

In other words, with the bottle rolling, and him still bent down, I also dropped the ketchup. With the lid open. Also accidentally on purpose. Clumsy me.

Time seemed to freeze in that instant, as the bottle flew and thick gobs of red splattered across the checkerboard pattern that traversed his superior derriere. He jumped. I screeched. And the ketchup bottle joined the mustard bottle on the floor.

"I'm so sorry!" I yelped.

He looked over his shoulder at the crimson mess that was his ass. "It's, um, OK," he said, not looking the least bit OK. "Accidents happen."

I paused. Poor thing looked so innocent. "Fuck," I lamented, feeling about as guilty as a cat that'd just eaten a canary—after he dipped it in ketchup.

He grinned. "Yeah, I think we covered that earlier."

I shook my head. "Different fuck," I admitted. "See, it's been a really, really, *really* bad week. Taylor Swift would've had a field day with it, in fact."

"I gathered," he said, reaching for some paper towels, which did little to clean up the mess, apart from turning his pants red and my cheeks even redder.

"And, well," I added, "I sort of dropped the ketchup on purpose."

He paused, seemingly to mull over what I'd said. "Why, to see if it was breakable?" He lifted up the bottle and tapped the plastic. "Nope."

And still my head moved from side to side. "Um, no, not exactly," I said sheepishly. "More like to see you take your slacks off." And my blush went all supernova on me. "Again, Tom, I'm so, so sorry. This isn't like me, honestly. Breakups and booze don't mix well, you see."

Once more he paused, then reached down and retrieved the mustard. He then grabbed a hold of the elastic waistband of his checkerboard slacks, yanked them down, and promptly pulled them over his work clogs. "All better now?"

My heart momentarily ceased to beat, my mouth just as suddenly Saharan. "Much," I croaked out, a bead of sweat trickling down my forehead despite the fact that the kitchen was quite cool.

He had runner's legs, thin and hairy, etched to perfection, culminating in a jock-covered pouch that I ached to dive into, very kangaroo-like. "Now can I start cooking our dinner?" he asked, staring at me as I stared (gaped, gazed, gawked) at him. "The fish isn't going to cook itself, you know."

I nodded. "Um, yeah, sure," I replied. "Can I watch?" I left out the *in rapt delight* part.

His smile returned, a wink thrown in for good measure. "Suit yourself," he replied, back to business now, "you're the boss." He turned and started his prep work, ass jiggling, gloriously framed as it was in the white elastic. "And hand me the fish, please. It's on the cart inside the ice chest."

I looked away, however reluctantly, and did as he'd said. I grabbed the ziplocked fish from the chest and placed it on the counter, then stood next to him, inhaled, and, finally, rested my hand on his exposed ass. Naughty me.

He snickered and slightly turned his face my way. "Um, what-cha doin'?"

"You said I was the boss," I replied, hesitantly, though keeping my hand right where it was. "I believe this is what's called *quality control.*" I fondled the left cheek, then the right, my fingers tracing the hairy crack. "Quality." I gazed at my trembling hand on his beguiling rump. *"Check."*

He nodded and widened his stance as he started to arrange his work station, removing things from the tray and laying them down this way and that. "I think you missed a spot."

I moved from his side to his back and crouched down, ass to face. I craned my neck up and took a deep whiff of him. He smelled of musk and sweat, with just a hint of cinnamon. I grabbed his alabaster cheeks and pried them apart. His hair-rimmed hole winked out at me, pink and puckered and utterly perfect. "Grade-A prime," I rasped. "Also *check.*"

He looked over his shoulder. "A cursory inspection is fine, sir," he informed. "But a taste test is mandated before you can actually sign off on it."

My gulp made its triumphant return. "Really?"

He started dicing and slicing. "Says so in the culinary handbook."

Well, far be it from me to argue with a man with a sharp knife in his hand, I figured. In other words, I moved in another inch, craned my neck even further, and gave his hole an ample tasting. My tongue licked and lapped and zoomed around his chute before I dove it in. He moaned appreciatively, the sound interspersed with that of the knife as it deftly minced and shred. *Chop, chop, lick. Chop, chop, lick.*

"Hmm," I eventually hummed, halfway through my rather wet ministrations.

The knife went silent. *"Hmm,* what?"

I moved my mouth slightly away from his rump. "You gonna stuff that sea bass of yours, Tom?"

He shrugged. "I was thinking about it," he informed. "Maybe with a nice crab mix. I brought some along, just in case."

"I see," I said, already one depraved step ahead of him. "So why should the fish have all the stuffing fun?"

He barely seemed to give it a moment's thought before a medium-sized cucumber got dropped to the floor. "Well, I do like to get my recommended daily allotment of vegetables," he quipped. "Guess we'll just be skipping the digesting part."

I grabbed the cucumber, then stared from it to his rather tight hole. Realizing that one was far larger than the other, I hopped up and searched for a means to an end. That is to say, I hopped up and found what was needed to stuff his end.

"Olive oil all right?" I asked, slathering the green vegetable with it as I again crouched down.

"Extra virgin?" he asked, continuing with his prep work, barely giving me a look.

I shrugged. "But of course." I then dribbled the oil onto the end of my fingers and rubbed it onto him—round and round he goes—before gliding one, two, and, finally, three slicked up digits in and up and back. Tom moaned and groaned and stood on clogged tippy toes as I entered him, back arching as he let out a ferocious exhale. "Everything OK?" I asked, staring up at him.

He seemed to gather his wits about him before replying. "Right as rain."

I took his word for it, especially since he was again working diligently on our meal, the knife but a blur in his capable hands. My fingers came out with an audible *pop*. Tom's clogs again rested on the tile floor. And as for that rigid cucumber, it was now pressed up tight to his oiled-up hole. "Still raining?" I asked, just in case.

He nodded. "Pouring," he groaned, rapturously, as I slowly, easily, gently, slid the phallic veggie up his portal. Pouring, suffice it to say, quickly gave way to purring. *"Niiice."*

In and out the cucumber slid, the smell of sex and oil wafting languidly up my nostrils. From my vantage point, I couldn't see what Tom was up to, except that his free hand had obviously worked its way inside the front of the jock all of a sudden. So, best guess, he was now dicing, slicing, and jacking, very ambidextrously, away.

"Need any help?" I thought to ask.

"With which part?" he rasped.

I grinned. "Well, since I'm already down here ..."

In other words, with the cucumber buried in deep and not going anywhere, I relieved my personal chef of his personal undies. Tom lifted each of his clogged feet until his lower half was naked, midsection ramming and jamming against the cabinets. I then pushed myself between his legs, back up against wood, and stared up at a rather fetching pair of low-hangers and a cock that could crack open a coconut—no, not a figure of speech; he'd actually brought a coconut with him.

"*Niiice,*" I echoed.

He pushed his dick down. I raised my neck up. We met in the middle, his wide, helmeted head and my eager mouth joining as one. In his thick meat went, a happy gagging tear meandering its way down my cheek as he coaxed it further inside my throat. All the while, I tugged and torqued and twisted and yanked on his heavy, hanging balls with one hand, the other reaching betwixt his legs to push and shove that faux dildo in and out, in and out.

"Wait, wait!" he suddenly barked.

I popped his prick out of my mouth and, for the moment, stopped pummeling his ass with the salad-wannabe. "For?" I asked.

He stared down at me, eyes of blue sparkling like sapphires. "Too close."

"And?" I slapped his prick against my wet lips.

"I have an idea," he panted in reply.

I moved my head up and licked his balls, sweat hitting the back of my throat like a bullet. "Well, thus far your ideas have panned out well." I stared up at him. "Shoot."

"I plan on it," he replied. "While we're eating. *And* while you're fucking me."

I squinted his way. "You're joking."

He shook his head. "Never about food, boss." He grinned. "Or fucking, for that matter."

Suddenly, I'd completely forgotten about my ex-boyfriend. Again, go figure. "You're on." To which I added, and rightly so, "Or maybe make that *in.*"

182

Just over an hour later, I found myself at the dinner table. Such an innocuous statement, huh? Especially since I found myself at the dinner table in nothing but a lubed-up rubber and a radiant smile on my face—not to mention a gurgle in my belly, because I was actually starving by that point.

As for Tom, he strode in, silver tray in hand, clogs on his feet, and absolutely nothing else. Thankfully, I wasn't drinking at the time, or a spit-take would've been quick to follow. See, Tom was stunning from the waist down, that much I already knew, but take away all the rest of it, and my top chef was literally tops, however quick to bottom he soon would be.

"Wow," I squeaked out.

He grinned. "Yep, dinner did turn out quite well, if I do say so myself."

I shook my head. *"So* not what I was referring to, dude."

His grin widened. "Ah …"

"Yeah, *ah.*" I pointed at my ramrod stiff prick. "Now have a seat—*we're* famished."

He moved quickly, stupendous cock swaying all the while. Back and forth from the kitchen he went, setting down our food, our drinks—and the rubber and bottle of lube I'd already given him—until the table was perfect, the meal delectable looking, company very much included.

"Now I lay me down to feast," I said, eyeing it all hungrily.

He chuckled. "Wrong prayer," he said. "And incorrect."

I shrugged. "But it's the only one I could think of with the word *lay* in it …"

He nodded and strode over to me. "You have a point."

I aimed my finger at my swollen, throbbing prick. "Indeed I do."

He leaned over and sheathed the beast before lubing it and him up. As for the *amuse-bouche,* the appetizer before the appetizer that came in the offering of his lips upon mine, which was about as close to landing on a cloud as a guy could get—or maybe make that a bowl of mashed potatoes, which were placed barely a foot from my plate. Some heavy spit was swapped before we got down to the task, not to mention the meal, at hand.

"*Niiice,*" he eventually whispered into my mouth.

"Yep, I believe we've already covered that," I replied.

"Bears repeating," said he as he positioned his stellar rump just above my aching prick. Down he went, a moan escaping from between his lips, a groan from mine. "*Bon appétit,*" he then added.

"Emphasis on the boning," I remarked as we both stared at the glorious meal set before us, candlelight twinkling in the center of it all, flowers adjusted just right.

Down I chowed, and down his ass went, grinding into my lap until my cock felt like it would explode. Up our glasses went, clinking together, and up his ass went, sending a million volts of electricity through my extremities.

"Delicious," he sighed, chewing on the exquisitely prepared sea bass.

"Amen," I reverently uttered, stroking his cock as I devoured my meal with gusto. "Compliments to the chef."

He nodded and leaned his head back for a kiss. "Nice to have an appreciative audience." Which meant that gross understatements officially traveled in threes.

And so this is how we proceeded, bon mots passed as freely as the wine and the excellent food, with him riding my cock all the while. Was it weird to be eating with a perfect stranger on my lap? Well, since the stranger was indeed perfect and since he was more in my lap than on my lap, we'll still go with yes, weird—but with a *nicely* placed before it. In fact, the only difficulty, apart from eating in such close quarters, was not cumming. I mean, with him I could just stop pumping and stroking; for me, there was always an extra tight tush gripping my pole, practically pulling the cum up from my balls.

In other words, though the food was five-star, we still ate it fast, eager for the inevitable outcome, which was rapidly rising like the soufflé in the oven.

So with plates soon bare and glasses empty, I picked up the pace on his cock, which had barely flagged since we'd started. It pulsed and thickened in my sweaty grip as his head leaned back into mine, his mouth in a pant.

"Ready?" I whispered into his ear, taking a bite of the lobe that was just as tender as the fish we'd delightfully consumed.

"Uh-huh," he moaned in reply, the vibration strumming through us both.

"Thank God," I replied, my ass bucking with abandon now, hand doing the same, our bodies a sticky, united tangle.

And then, at last, his back arched and his cock exploded, thick bands of gooey, aromatic cum spewing up before raining down on my good china. He moaned loudly as he shot and shot, my tablecloth sure to never be the same again. Though that was the farthest thought from my head as his hole clenched tightly around my prick, sending me into overdrive. Which meant that as he came, so did I, filling his ass and that rubber up with a heavy load of my own.

"*Fuuuck*," I exhaled, every nerve ending in my body suddenly on fire.

He chuckled as I shook the last vestiges of opalescent spooge from his cock. "Yeah, I think we just did."

I wrapped my arms around his narrow waist. "I'll never look at a piece of fish the same way again."

He sighed, contentedly. "I aim to please."

I looked over his shoulder, at the postprandial mess he'd made. "And your aim is spot on." I strummed his taught belly and ran my fingers through a trail of spunk he'd left behind. "But perhaps we should extricate ourselves before my cock becomes permanently welded to your spectacular hole."

He ran his hands over mine. "I could think of worse things, boss."

I paused, letting the implication sink in. "So you'd like a, uh, repeat then."

He didn't need a pause. "Well, there is enough food to last for days you know." He locked his hand on top of mine. "Plus, someone needs to get fucked during the dessert." He turned his head my way and added a cherry to the topping. "That Jefferson guy clearly didn't know a good thing when he had one."

Fucking ex-boyfriend didn't know his ass from his elbow, let alone how to cook a Chilean sea bass—with a cucumber rammed up his chute, no less. Talk about multitasking. "Jefferson who?" I cooed.

"Exactly," he retorted, cock already starting its upward climb. "Now let's clean up."

But still I held him tight. "Nah, forget about it," I said. "I have a feeling it's just going to get a whole lot messier all too soon."

"Amen to that," he moaned.

"Amen to that, indeed."

186

MOVING OUT WITH A BANG

J.R. Haney

Misery. Well, actually Missouri, but sometimes it's tough to tell the difference. It's a ninety degree day; the humidity is through the roof and today, of all days, is the day I chose to move to my new loft. I truly couldn't have picked a worse day to move out of this apartment. Lucky for me, I'll just be giving orders today. I hired a moving company to do that heavy lifting for me. Meanwhile, I'll be lounging around going through financial reports in my gym clothes.

I might be a credit analyst that sits at a desk all day, but one thing I won't let the chair do is waste away at my body. I still make it to the gym and keep myself in shape. I'm not ripped by any means of the word, but I do have some definition. I don't want to look like a 'roided up gay, just one that takes care of himself. Honestly, I think I'm pretty average. Six feet tall and 190 pounds. It's rare that anyone sees me as a threat or takes a second glance, at least from the front. I mean, I've never heard complaints; I'm packing a solid seven inches, cut, but I certainly don't parade my dick around. Still, I like my body. And my ass is rockin'. It's the one thing I'm really proud of: a nice bubble butt that leaves nothing to the imagination, especially in the shorts I'm wearing today.

As I'm sitting at my desk going through the latest batch of loan paperwork, I hear a knock at the door. I make my way down the hall of my apartment and open the door. There he stands in shorts and a tank top that looks like it's one size too small. He stands about six-foot-two, I'd say, and his cocky grin tells me that he knows his tank top is too small. But clearly it's meant to showcase his impressive buffed-out bod. I might have definition, but this guy lives at the gym apparently.

"Hi, I'm Todd. Are you the one moving?" Short, sweet, and to the point. I can appreciate that. Hopefully that's his modus operandi across the board, which will make the move will go quickly and efficiently. I don't want to be out in this weather, and I'm sure he doesn't either.

"Yeah, that's me. Come on in, I'll show you what you're moving … Are there more of you?"

The response is a very flat "No." Again, short and sweet, but I'd say the personality is a bit lacking. God, he's lucky he's pretty. "Other guy didn't show up."

"How do you plan to move this furniture?" I ask. "I really didn't plan on helping—that's why I hired you." His face is blank, and I'm not sure if my comment has pissed him off or if he simply doesn't comprehend what I'm saying. "Will you at least drop your … rate?"

Thank God I stopped myself; I really wanted to say *pants*. The bulge protruding from his shorts is unfathomable. Maybe he's a shower, not a grower. Regardless, there doesn't seem to be anything small about Todd. I would love to ship *his* goods right to the back of my throat.

"Sure," he says. "As long as you help, I'll give you a deep discount." I think he might be picking up on my innuendo—and I haven't even been laying it on that thick.

We start to pick up and move the furniture to the back of the moving truck. More often than I would like to admit, I find myself staring at Todd as he lifts. He moves with such ease. It doesn't take much effort for him to throw things around. It seems like I'm not doing a lot of the work really—I'm just there to steer furniture and boxes around corners and through doors. The truck fills up fast, but we never lose the pace.

As Todd starts to pick up a box, I notice the sweat gleaming off his bulging biceps and I see his legs strain under the weight of my smaller workout supplies. "Only one room left," I tell him. My voice reveals a little too much excitement. This is the room I've been waiting for. "I need some help taking the bed frame apart. It really isn't a one-person job."

As we move from the living room down the hall to my bedroom—a trek that few men have made lately—I feel my cock start to rise. For most of the day I've been trying to keep my mind focused on the task at hand. But every time I look at Todd, my cock perks up and I have to keep my excitement from showing through my shorts. Now, though, it seems to be beyond my control; my cock has decided to think for itself. Before we even reach the bedroom door, my prick is standing at attention. My mind is racing, trying to find something else to focus on …

And then I feel a rough, hard hand against the right cheek of my ass. "Before we do that … are you still wanting that discount?" His voice is quiet but direct.

I must have been more flirtatious than I realized. Somehow he knows it was his pants I'd wanted him to drop and not his rate. Even though we had barely communicated all day. And to be honest, I thought he was pretty dull, one of those "me so pretty, let's fuck" sorts. Not only that, I couldn't imagine he'd be all that interested. Sure I'm in shape, but nothing like this guy. When you put the two of us next to one another, there's no question which one of us sits at a desk all day.

"I think a discount is justified," I manage.

"Do you now …?"

I turn around and look him in the eye, and he smirks at me. I watch as he grabs his dick through his shorts, and I can't help but notice that he's packing a very girthy member. "Like I said, I'll give you a deep discount," he says, putting his other hand on my shoulder. I feel the pressure of his arm pushing me down to my knees.

When the day started, I thought *I'd* be the one giving the orders—yet here I sit, on my knees, looking Todd's appendage starting to protrude from the top of his shorts. I like what I'm seeing. His piss slit is barely visible but I can tell it's covered by quite a bit of foreskin. It looks fucking tasty. I can't wait to wrap my tongue around that mushroom of his. His cock is at least eight solid inches. And thick. So thick. Tree trunk thick. It's going to require some work on my part, but I already know it will be worth the effort.

I stretch out the band of his shorts to get a full view of his fully erect dick and proceed to pull his shorts down, past his knees, and slip them off over his shoes. When I finally get my hand around his beer can cock, I realize that comparing it to a beer can is actually not that far off. He's thick and he knows it. I look up and see a sly smirk coming from Todd as he grips the base and pushes the tip of his cock head on my lips. As he pulls his dick up from my bottom lip, I see a line of pre-cum follow his slit up until it finally disconnects and I feel it snap back to my lip. I lick my lips, partially to get ready for the beast that's about to invade my mouth, but more to get a taste of his appetizing seed. Before I can finish, I feel his calloused hand grab the hair on the back of my head and start to push my head forward.

I expect a slow start to give my mouth time to adjust and work its way around his meaty tool, but I quickly learn that's not what Todd has in mind. Before I even have time to take a breath, my nose is buried in his thick bush. I breathe in deep through my nose and take in his sweaty musk. I savor his sweet man scent as his hand pulls back on my hair, forcing me to release the bone that I want so badly to keep buried in me.

As the pressure from his hand returns to the back of my head, I hear him moan when my lips again engulf his mass. "Fuck, man," he grunts. "Your mouth feels fuckin' great. Hope you're ready for a workout." The cocky son-of-a-bitch. *Now* he's able to manage full sentences.

"Yes," I mumble through the muzzle that is his member, slurring my speech and making it damned near impossible to give any more of an answer.

His hand starts to pick up the pace, making my head bob back and forth. "More tongue," he demands. I happily oblige and proceed to swirl my licker under his foreskin and around his head. "We aren't stopping here," he states. And before I have time to comprehend his words, he yanks my head off his dick and pushes me down onto the bed.

"What are you doing?" I yelp more than ask. It's all I want to know, really. He's teasing me, the fucker. He's been in charge from the get-go, but I'm not one to move ahead without a plan.

Before I even finish the question, I see his too-small shirt hit the floor. The shoes quickly follow. "You're cleaning my balls now, bitch," he laughs and rushes at the bed. I lie back and wait to enjoy the ride. The rigid muscles from his thighs strain against the side of my face, and as his ball sac rests on my chin, I work my tongue around his right testicle. It's hanging slightly lower, so I take the nugget into my mouth and work it over with my tongue. His balls are smooth and delicious.

It doesn't take long for the next order to emerge from his lips. "Take them both," he demands, "my workout isn't for pussies." It's like this man is reading my mind. I stretch my mouth and work both of his jewels gently into my throat. Meanwhile, my own cock is practically begging to be set free from the confines of my shorts. Todd's demands are making me rock hard. Having someone take over in the bedroom is my biggest turn-on.

I've had plenty of fantasies in my day, each one a little raunchier than the last. Yet I maintain control in most areas of my life. It comes from work. Everything there is black and white. There isn't a gray and you don't cross the line very often. I like being able to make those decisions, and it's this structure that keeps me sane. However, years ago, I had a "daddy" type take control of me sexually, and afterwards I was never the same. From that day forward, every time I tried to dominate in the bedroom, the experience was lackluster.

Todd is anything but lackluster. His stern demands and cocky attitude have my rod at attention for him. While I'm busy making sure his balls are squeaky clean, he moves his hand down my stomach and grips my meat hard. *"Ow!"* I pull my head away from his balls and yelp as his monstrous hand clamps down on my rigid cock.

He grins. "What's the matter, bitch? That hurt? You better get back to working my balls …"

As I continue slathering his nuggets, he grabs his monster and starts slapping me across the forehead with it. I reach my hand down my shorts and work the pre-cum around the head of my aching cock while my mouth moans into his sac.

"Keep doing it, you little prick," Todd hisses.

I stroke my sausage up and down using the pre-cum, which is now dripping from my piss slit, as my own personal lubricant, all the while continuing to moan into my pliable skin microphone, sending tremors through Todd's body.

He better not burst—I'm not leaving here without walking funny. As much as I want to taste his man seed, I would much rather have my insides coated with it. I want that cock in my ass. And I decide it's best to be straightforward about this.

"I want you in me," I say.

He gives me the smirk. It makes him look evil, but it makes me throb with excitement. "I'll stretch your little man pussy out in good time. You need to learn some patience, bitch."

Yes, please, I think. And with that, I find myself on my stomach. He pulls my shorts down to my ankles, leaving my stark white underwear exposed.

"How old are you?" he asks, practically giggling. "Grown men shouldn't be wearing tighty-whities." *Smack.* His firm hand makes direct contact with my right ass cheek. *Smack.* Again. Not only does it make my cock surge, my ass is now pulsing with excitement as well. I have never been more aroused.

"Please give it to me. I need it." I sound so pathetic. But I want him to impale me. I want him to stretch my hole and make me his little bitch. And I want it now.

As if my begging isn't pathetic enough, it's then that I hear a rip. Looking over my shoulder, I see Todd's face light up as his determined fingers force a hole through the fabric of my underwear. Through the tear, he traces my ass crack with the tip of his pointer from top to bottom, paying extra attention to my smooth hole. He leans down and I feel his breath on me as his hands grab each of my ass cheeks and spread them apart. He starts running his tongue from the top of my crevice; it probes around my hole before he buries his face in deep, nibbling and grinding his scruffy face into my rosebud, his unyielding tongue prying its way deeper and deeper into my man pocket.

"Fuck, yes!" I scream and push my ass back into his face. His arms wrap around my thighs and pull me in tighter. His grip tightens to keep me from squirming. I reach back and put my hand on the back on his head, urging him to dig deep for my treasure. His mouth is relentless.

"You taste awesome," he says between lashes from his thick tongue. "I'm going to tear you apart."

I feel his face disconnect from my ass and, without missing a beat, I feel his shaft work its way between my mounds. He's teasing me and I can't take it. "Fuck me!" I demand. "Ram that dick into me! I want to feel every inch of you sliding into my ass!"

He moves the head of his cock toward my hole and I feel the pressure as he starts to work it in. I turn my head around just in time to see the ball of spit drop from his mouth down to the split in my cheeks. I feel it run down until it finally hits his cock and he rubs it in for lube. My cock throbs and drips in anticipation of his entry.

"Fuck!" I scream out. I know the neighbors on the floor below me can hear it but I'm moving, so what do I care? Todd doesn't waste time. My need for his cock must seem urgent because he slams his rod right into me. I feel every inch and it's sheer pain. As I wriggle my ass around, trying to get at least a little bit of his thick tool out of me, his hands grab my hips and pull me right back on. *Relax,* I think. This experience may never come again. *Enjoy it.* Todd slips his massive member out of my ass and within seconds he slams himself right back in, causing another cursing episode. But the initial shock of his girth has gone away.

I'm ready to play his game.

I pull myself completely up onto the bed and he follows suit. Drawing myself up onto my hands and knees, I push myself back into that perfect V he has leading to his crotch. "So, you want it, do you?" he asks. Again with that cocky little grin.

"Yes, I want it. Fuck me hard—please, sir," I beg. "My cock is dripping for you. I want your load. I want to take that seed deep into me." There's a sense of humiliation that comes from begging for his dick but I surrendered my dignity to Todd back when he forced me down on my knees.

He pulls his cock all the way out, which leaves me feeling surprisingly empty. In shock, I turn around. "What the fuck are you doing?" I ask.

"I know you want it," he says with a snarl, "so you're not gettin' it. *Yet.* Now get on your back." I flip over as he grabs a rag from the floor and wipes his dick down. "Now turn around. I want your head over the side of the bed, bitch. I'm making you mine." I do as he commands and hang my head off the side of the bed, mouth open and awaiting a deposit.

Without hesitation, Todd rams his cock in and all the way to the back of my throat. I feel the heat practically radiating from his balls against my nose. He pumps himself deep into my throat and I taste the savory pre-cum running from his spigot. He moans as I snake my tongue around his dick, matching him thrust for thrust. His abs are getting rigid and I hear his breathing start to shorten. I think I'm about to get what I'm craving, but then he stops.

He pulls his dick away from my mouth and a steady stream of spit trails along with it until it finally releases and drops to my face. He laughs. "I wish you could see what a cum pig you look like right now. You look fuckin' crazed. You want my load, huh?"

Of course I do. I want his load. I was so close.

"It's your turn," he says. "I'll give you some attention now, since you've been so obedient." He removes my shirt first and then decides it's time to get rid of my mutilated underwear. He strokes my throbbing cock—it's about time—using my pre-cum as lube just as I had done. I moan and try to reach the bone floating above my face with the tip of my tongue. *Smack*. My cheek stings. "This is your time—enjoy it," Todd says, his voice low and full of authority. "You'll get your chance to wet my cock down for your ass. Don't you worry …"

The stroking of his calloused hand over my firm cock continues and I know I won't last much longer. Between the sight of his dick teasingly bouncing above my face, and the feel of his rough hand going up and down on my shaft, I can feel an eruption of epic proportions coming. Again, he must be reading my mind. Because as my breathing hastens, he grabs the base of his own cock and shoves it back in my mouth—once again aiming his thick mushroom head directly toward my throat—ceasing his assault on my now red member. As he rams his dick further and further in—it feels like it's gaining length, though I know that's not possible—it's clear to me that I'm lubing him up for the finale. Or at least I hope I am. He seems to be in a rage as he grabs my hair and pulls my head further off the bed. He lets my face have it. I only endure about thirty seconds of him plunging my throat before he pulls my head off his cock and gives my cheek a firm slap.

"You're mine now, bitch," he says as he grabs my legs and spins me around on the bed. He slaps my ass cheeks as he probes the head of his dick into my man pussy. He isn't playing anymore. There's none of that pulling-it-out-and-ramming-it-in-shit. He's going for gold, and I scream to let him know that he's going to win.

He pumps in and out of me hard. The whole bed is rattling and I'm fucking loving it. The sensation and the sound of his thighs

196

slapping against my ass turns me on even more. I reach my hand up and, for the first time, I feel his pecs. I give one of his nipples a quick twist, which gets precisely the reaction I'm hoping for. He looks at me, his gaze very stern, and again slaps me on the ass. "You don't touch me unless I tell you to. This isn't your show, whore." Damn, he's not kidding around.

As he continues to pound the living daylights out of me, I see his eyes light up as my cock starts to throb. Each one of his thrusts pushes perfectly against my prostate, and I can feel my cock start to spew. Without so much as a hand on my dick, I effortlessly cum with the force of Mount Vesuvius, creating a puddle of slimy happiness on my stomach. It's a first for me, and judging by the look on his face, it's a first for him, too. Before I can even finish, the contractions from my ass have Todd moaning.

"Oh fuck!" he yells as his cock pulses deep within me. I feel every shot being plowed into my ass, and I can tell it's a big load.

After the spasming ceases, Todd collapses on top of me. I can see the sweat glistening off the muscles in his back. After a few seconds he looks up at me, and I know what he's about to ask. "Does that happen to you often? Cumming without touching yourself, I mean?"

"No, that was a first for me," I say. "But I don't want it to be my last. I think this should happen more often. It's hard to find someone around here who can take control like you do."

As he pulls out of my ass and gets off the bed he says, "I think we can make that happen. It's not like I won't know where you live. Now let's get this finished. I want to help you christen the new place, too."

With that, we get dressed and then load the rest of the boxes into the truck. It doesn't take long. I want this move to be over, so I can help pleasure Todd again. "Follow me," I tell him as I make my way to my car.

I keep my eyes peeled on my rearview mirror all the way across town. He just smirks, knowing that I'm watching him. Fifteen minutes later, as I'm getting out of my car, I notice Todd is already parked and out of the truck—and his dick is clearly stiff, judging by the outline in his shorts. I stumble to find the keys to the new place as I head for the front door. I'm in such a rush that I drop my key ring.

As I bend over to pick it up, I sense a presence behind me. I feel Todd's hands wrap around my thighs and his massive prick finds its way between my ass cheeks through my shorts. As I begin to stand up, another hand pushes my head back down. "What you had before was just an appetizer, you pussy." It's a voice I don't recognize, but I instantly like its authoritative tone. "Now find that fucking key so we can get the party started …"

Could this be the mover who didn't show up this morning? Is he here to help Todd *unload?* In more ways than one? It seems round two is going to happen sooner than I thought. Only this time, I'm actually getting both the workers I paid for.

ABOUT THE EDITOR AND AUTHORS

Born and raised in Normal, Illinois, WINSTON GIESEKE began writing short stories and plays at a young age to escape the banality of a healthy Midwestern upbringing. He relocated to Los Angeles at eighteen and received a degree in screenwriting from California State University, Northridge, three years later. Kickstarting his career as a television writer, he penned episodes for shows like *Wildfire* and *Hollywood Off-Ramp* as well as the made-for-cable movie *Romantic Comedy 101*, which starred Tom Arnold and Joey Lawrence. He composed tantalizing copy for various adult entertainment companies (including Penthouse.com and Napali Video, home of "big boobs and catfights") and served as editor in chief of both *Men* and *Freshmen* magazines before honing his journalistic skills as managing editor of *The Advocate*. An award-seeking vocalist whose "rich voice harkens back to vintage Hollywood crooners" (Gay.net), his "saucy yet heartfelt" debut album, *On the Edge*, which "takes classic material, turns it upside down, and then spits it out with panache" (*Frontiers*), was released in 2012. He spent two years in Berlin, an experience he shamelessly exploited at ExpatsInBerlin.us, and now resides somewhere in southern California. He is the editor of the anthologies *Indecent Exposures*, *Daddy Knows Best*, *Straight No More*, *Blowing Off Class*, *Whipping Boys*, and *Until the Sun Rises*, *Out of Uniform*, and the Lambda Literary Award finalist *Team Players*.

DAVID APRYS is a formerly innocent ex-altar boy. Originally from the Midwest, he's lived in southern California, London, and the Deep South. He now makes his home near the Chesapeake Bay. An unrepentant hedonist and keen observer of people, he's worn the hats of investigator, freelance magazine writer, and actor in his varied professional life. The author of several erotic stories published in Bruno Gmünder anthologies, he's currently hard at work on his first novel, *Changeling*.

The author of several books—including the private eye novel *All White Girls*—MICHAEL BRACKEN is better known as the author of almost 1,000 short stories, including erotic fiction published in *Best Gay Erotica 2013, Flesh & Blood: Guilty as Sin, Freshmen, Hot Blood: Strange Bedfellows, Men, Model Men, Sexy Sailors, The Mammoth Book of Best New Erotica 4, The Mammoth Book of Erotic Confessions, Ultimate Gay Erotica 2006*, and many others. He lives and writes in Texas.

LANDON DIXON's writing credits include the magazines *Men, Freshmen, [2], Mandate, Torso,* and *Honcho;* stories in the anthologies *Straight? Volume 2, Friction 7, Working Stiff, I Like It Like That, Black Fire, Boy Fun, The Sweeter the Juice, Big Holiday Packages, Best of Both, Brief Encounters, Hot Daddies, Hot Jocks, Black Dungeon Masters, Indecent Exposures, Team Players, Ultimate Gay Erotica 2005, 2007,* and *2008,* and *Best Gay Erotica 2009;* and the short story collections *Hot Tales of Gay Lust 1, 2* and *3.*

RYAN FIELD is the author of over 100 published works of fiction, the best-selling *Virgin Billionaire* series, a romance featured on the Home Shopping Network, *Loving Daylight,* and a few more works of full length fiction with a pen name. His work has been in

Lambda Award-winning anthologies. You can reach him here at www.ryan-field.blogspot.com or at rfieldj@aol.com.

Known mostly for her erotic fiction, which has come out with publishers worldwide, P.A. FRIDAY also writes regularly about disability and about the Regency Period (both interests often seep into her erotica), and has been known to branch out and write about almost anything! She hates coffee, drinks too much red wine, has an unnervingly large collection of *Doctor Who* DVDs, and blogs at PenelopeFriday.LiveJournal.com.

J.R. HANEY is a writer from small-town Missouri with an avid imagination and a hunger to learn all he can regarding sex. His writing combines many personal experiences with a splash of fantasy to spice it up for himself and his readers alike.

JEFFREY HARTINGER is a native of Buffalo, New York. After graduating from college, he moved to Los Angeles and began writing for *The Advocate*. He writes about comedy, current events, politics, and the LGBT rights movement on his Web site, www.thewhygenerationusa.blogspot.com. He currently lives in New York City.

MIKE HICKS is the pseudonym of a writer and editor whose fiction has appeared in the magazines *Men*, *Freshmen*, *[2]*, *Inches*, *Honcho*, *Unzipped*, *Torso*, *Playguy*, and *Mandate*, and on the Web site of the graphic artist Patrick Fillion, where he chronicled the interplanetary erotic adventures of the characters Camili-Cat and Naked Justice. He lives with his partner in Boston, Massachusetts.

T. HITMAN is the nom de porn of a professional writer whose short fiction appeared in *Men*, *Freshmen*, and *Torso*, among others. For five years, he also wrote the *Unzipped* Web review column and contributed hundreds of interviews and feature articles on some of the hottest men in the gay porn industry.

BRETT LOCKHARD is a writer who lives in New York City with a bunch of succulents.

GREGORY L. NORRIS lives and writes in the outer limits of New Hampshire. He once worked as a screenwriter on two episodes of Paramount's *Star Trek: Voyager* and is the author of the handbook to all things Sunnydale, *The Q Guide to Buffy the Vampire Slayer*. Norris writes regularly for various national magazines and fiction anthologies, and is a judge on 2012's Lambda Awards. Visit him online at www.gregorylnorris.blogspot.com.

ABNER RAY is a California-based writer who originally hails from South Carolina. He enjoys intense mountain biking, painting water colors, and collecting vintage French postcards.

ROB ROSEN (www.therobrosen.com), award-winning author of the novels *Sparkle: The Queerest Book You'll Ever Love*, *Divas Las Vegas*, *Hot Lava*, *Southern Fried*, *Queerwolf*, and *Vamp*, and editor of the anthologies *Lust in Time* and *Men of the Manor*, has had short stories featured in more than 180 anthologies.

NATTY SOLTESZ's novel *Backwoods* was a 2012 Lambda Literary Award finalist and features illustrations by Michael Kirwan. His stories have been published in magazines like *Freshmen* and *Mandate* and in anthologies like *Best Gay Erotica 2011* and *Best*

Gay Romance 2010. He co-wrote the screenplay for the 2009 Joe Gage-directed porn film *Dad Takes a Fishing Trip*. He lives in Pittsburgh, Pennsylvania.

From Lust to Love

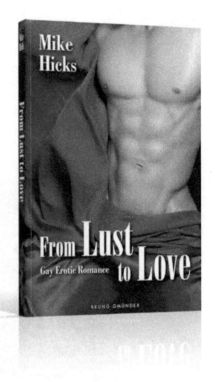

Mike Hicks
FROM LUST TO LOVE
Gay Erotic Romance
192 pages, softcover,
13 x 19 cm, 5¼ x 7½",
978-3-86787-790-9
US$ 16.99 / £ 10.99
€ 14,99

They meet at the bar. Or in the shower at the gym. And there's an instant connection. An unmistakable desire. He'll do for tonight, each thinks. But yet there's a spark of something more, something beyond passion. Something neither will admit they've been longing for. Could this be their last one-nighter? What happens when a casual hook-up satisfies your ultimate craving? That's when you go from lust to love ...

Gay Erotica at Its Best

Winston Gieseke (Ed.)
UNTIL THE SUN RISES
Gay Vampire Erotica
208 pages, softcover,
13 x 19 cm, 5¼ x 7½",
978-3-86787-691-9
US$ 17.99 / £ 11.99
€ 16,95

Winston Gieseke (Ed.)
WHIPPING BOYS
Gay S/M Erotica
208 pages, softcover,
13 x 19 cm, 5¼ x 7½",
978-3-86787-689-6
US$ 17.99 / £ 11.99
€ 16,95

Winston Gieseke (Ed.)
BLOWING OFF CLASS
Gay College Erotica
208 pages, softcover
13 x 19 cm, 5¼ x 7½"
978-3-86787-686-5
US$ 17.99 / £ 11.99 / € 15,95

Gay Erotica at Its Best

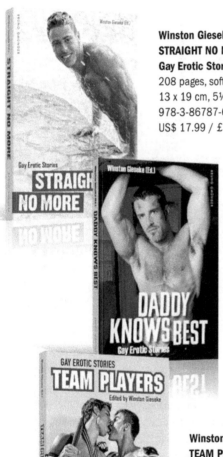

Winston Gieseke (Ed.)
STRAIGHT NO MORE
Gay Erotic Stories
208 pages, softcover,
13 x 19 cm, 5¼ x 7½",
978-3-86787-607-0
US$ 17.99 / £ 11.99 / € 16,95

Winston Gieseke (Ed.)
DADDY KNOWS BEST
Gay Erotic Stories
208 pages, softcover
13 x 19 cm, 5¼ x 7½"
978-3-86787-590-5
US$ 17.99 / £ 11.99 / € 15,95

Winston Gieseke (Ed.)
TEAM PLAYERS
Gay Erotic Stories
208 pages, softcover
13 x 19 cm, 5¼ x 7½"
978-3-86787-609-4
US$ 17.99 / £ 11.99 / € 15,95

Gayma Sutra

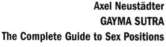
Axel Neustädter
GAYMA SUTRA
The Complete Guide to Sex Positions
192 pages, softcover,
13 x 19 cm, 5¼ x 7½",
978-3-86787-792-3
US$ 19.99 / £ 12.99
€ 14,99

In, over and out? Not with the **Gayma Sutra**!
This richly illustrated guide book will help spice up your sex life. More
variety means more fun, and the variations are just about endless.
Axel Neustädter has tested all the ways to play and found the ones to give
you all the pleasure you've always wanted. He answers crucial questions
about the most exciting sport there is: How to practice for the longest and
most intense sex? What are the best positions for masturbation? How can
two bottoms have an over-the-top experience together? And what toys can
help make it even better?
After reading this book, sex will never be boring again!